A FIRE AT ROMANTICON

Also by H.L. Brooks

Red August – Shifters of Mahigan Falls, Book One

Red Archer – Shifters of Mahigan Falls, Book Two

Red Hunter – Shifters of Mahigan Falls, Book Three

House on Blue Raven Lane: The Case of the Ghost Bride –
Hawthorne Hollow, Book One (December 2024)

A FIRE AT ROMANTICON

H.L. BROOKS

Write Women Publish

Content Warnings

Infidelity
Self-esteem issues
Ageism
Sexual content
Alcohol use

Contents

ONE

Soggy Bottoms

Peach put the finishing décor touches on her little office corner in the basement, near the egress window. It was the largest window down there, and the only one that got even the tiniest amount of sunlight each morning. She balanced a couple of succulents in small terracotta pots on the window's slender sill, then hung a suncatcher to throw rainbows when the light filtered in during that magical twenty minutes around sunrise. She had further tried to cheer the gray cinder block cave by painting the walls yellow just behind the desk and around the window. It helped, a little.

Most exciting though, her desk now displayed an official Rose Ramble coffee mug and *I'm a Rambler* coaster to set it on. She was her favorite author, and though Peach only had room for one narrow bookshelf in her office nook, it was half filled with the works of Rose Ramble, who over the last twelve years or so had written at least forty volumes filled with longing, love, and happily ever afters.

Satisfied with her little space, Peach headed up the steep staircase, ducking a bit for the pipes overhead, and noticed the door at the end of the hallway to the garage was hanging open. She could also see the garage door was open, letting all of the air conditioning out. Or was it letting the hot air in? She never could decide. She imagined her husband Doug must have trudged in from working on the lawn, grabbed a beer, and forgot to close it on his way back out. She rolled her eyes and let out a huff as she went down the hall to pull the door shut, but then spied a couple of large boxes sitting on the concrete floor next to the utility sink. She stepped into the dusty garage to have a closer look.

Peach leaned over to read the labels, confirming her suspicion, and grunted in frustration. She stood up straight, tugged her gray tee back down over her ample, jegging-clad backside and took a moment, hoping to calm herself with a few deep breaths. *It's okay Peach, just count to ten. You can handle this,* she assured herself, but she didn't make it to ten. She only got as far as two before she marched over to the window that looked out on the backyard, threw it open and yelled at the top of her lungs.

"Doug!" She could see her husband was just about to start up the mower. She shouted louder, "Doug!"

This time his head swiveled and he stood up straight, his baggy yellow shorts sagging to his knees. He put his hands on his hips, then held out his hands in a "what" expression. Her face now red and sweaty, Peach stomped out of the garage as best she could in her thin foam flip-flops and went around back.

"When did those book boxes arrive?" she demanded. Doug looked confused, then struck a defensive pose.

"I dunno. Last month I guess." He said it plainly, but there was a thread of tension beneath it. She stared at him a long while in disbelief. He unclenched, but then ran a gangly nervous hand through his sweaty hair without disturbing the slick on his pale damp forehead.

Finally, after another long breath to calm herself, she said, "Why didn't you tell me they came? And why are they all wet on the bottom?"

"I was in a hurry when they got here, on my way to karate. I meant to bring them in when I got back …"

"Yes, and?"

"And … I just forgot."

"But why are they all wet?"

"Who knows? I wasn't thinking about it, I just sat 'em down. Maybe a puddle from when I cleaned my car mats?"

Peach stood in silence, absorbing and nodding. A lump caught in her throat, her face flushed, and she swallowed down some tears. She was more angry than hurt, but also totally unsurprised, which was its own kind of hurt.

"You knew I was waiting for those books. You knew I needed to send those to the hotel a week ago. This feels intentional, Doug."

Doug let out a huff. "Oh, here we go. Like I'm trying to ruin your life. It's just a goddam hobby, babe." He gave her a dismissive wave. "Okay, you want me to feel bad about an accident? Fine—I screwed up. I'm a terrible person. I forgot to say a damn package arrived."

"Right," was all she said, her face unmoving as she glared, then turned and walked away.

"Peach! Come on, don't be such a drama queen. They're probably fine."

She went back to the garage as the mower started up and got out a box cutter, carefully sliced the tape and opened the box. It wasn't the Instagrammable, TikTokable unboxing moment she'd hoped for, like the ones she'd seen so many authors doing on their large granite counters in perfectly decorated kitchens. Or their home libraries, the walls lined with shelf after shelf of special editions and sprayed-edge books, character art and always a cushy seat. All dewy eyes and smiles as the look of accomplishment and joy washed over their faces—a moment Peach would always dream of as she scrolled her feeds in the middle of the night. Instead of fresh lipstick and a smiling face, she was sweaty and sad on the grubby damp garage floor. Instead of her friend Marny shooting video while she unboxed her first romance book—*Greyson Edging: Shades of Passion Series, Book One*—and popping open Prosecco to celebrate, she didn't even bother to take out her phone. What was the point?

Yet in spite of the circumstances and to her surprise, she felt a flash of excitement as she pulled a book—her book— out of the carton, and even felt a little proud of herself as she looked over the cover. A handsome man with windswept hair and a strong jawline was pulling loose his black and pink tie from his gray shirt, a bit of smooth and shapely pecs visible. His charcoal gray suit slacks were slipped just below his navel, the black leather belt unbuckled. And her name in tall bold letters, "Peach Kincaid." She felt a little dizzy with it all, and embarrassed at the same time. All she could think was, *What the hell am I doing? I'm not a writer! This is nuts!*

She rubbed her hand across the cover. Flipped its floppy pages and let the smell of "new book" kiss her nose. She considered the level of gumption it had taken her to get this far, and she had done it. She'd published a book. But she absolutely had no business publishing a book, and she certainly wasn't going to actually go to Romanticon anyway, so Doug probably did her a big favor by letting them languish here, getting wrinkled and ruined, and taking the agony of that decision away from her. She wouldn't have to admit she wasn't good enough to go; she just couldn't go because the books got ruined. That didn't hurt as much.

She grabbed a plastic lid from one of the Christmas bins and flipped it over to the clean side and started to pull out the books. The first layer was unscathed, maybe most of them were in sellable shape. Not that she was going to sell them, but it wouldn't hurt to look. They weren't cheap after all. The second layer didn't fare quite as well, about a third of them were damaged, the same for the next layer, but the entire bottom layer was ruined. Between the two boxes she had about eighteen unspoiled books. It was a sign—she should just stick to crochet.

Peach sighed. It was a good thing she was already meeting Marny for coffee.

TWO

Coffee Shop Revelations

O utside the coffee shop Peach caught a glimpse of her reflection in the window. She didn't even recognize herself anymore. With that persistent swath of gray hair she was tired of dyeing, her ill-fitting clothes, sensible shoes, and jowls—jowls for god's sake!—she saw her mother looking back at her. People had always thought Peach was ten years younger, up until last year. It was like those ten years had suddenly caught up to her all at once. Not that aging itself was a bad thing, but looking tired and used up and not giving one crap what you wore out of the house because it felt so pointless was probably not helping her confidence any.

She couldn't quite understand how it happened so fast, but she could pinpoint *when* it happened: when her last child headed off for college. It was as though she'd been holding so many things up, sucked in, smile on, that once she was alone with Doug she could finally see how much of her happiness came from absorbing herself into her children's lives. But now, with her nest empty and feeling at her worst, she would sit down and read romance book after romance book, her favorites all by Rose Ramble. It was so sweet to escape into a world where, whatever obstacles these women faced, they always ended up happy, and most of all, desired. She missed desire. Not just being desired, but that aching longing that comes with want of somebody. She had tried to have that with Doug, but every time she put on a new nightie or started to snuggle up to him he said he had work, or karate, or a football game to watch, or was just too tired. So she stopped trying. But she didn't stop wanting to feel desire.

She saw Marny's reflection appear over her shoulder, smiling.

"Hey, what's cookin' good-lookin'?"

"Ugh, I'm not feeling too good looking these days, Marn."

"Oh stop. You look …" Marny was thoughtful for a moment, her magenta-glossed lips pressing together while she came up with the right word. "… fine." Then she gave a strained smile.

Peach rolled her eyes. "Yeah, I know. I'm barely doing the basics anymore."

Marny's smile turned sympathetic and she reached out and gently touched her friend's forearm.

"Seriously though, Peach, you have not been looking like yourself lately, all shoulders slumped, bags under your eyes. Baggy—what are those, cutoff sweatpants?—baggy sweats, but not all cool like the Gen Zs wear them." She looked her over and nodded assertively. "You need sleep, sweetie. And a spa day and time to do something fun." She elbowed Peach. "Maybe a good railing?"

Peach let out an economical laugh and smiled at Marny, who looked stunning in her yellow sundress, with little bright pink patent leather slip-on sandals and matching handbag.

Her dark curly hair was decorated with a pink and yellow scarf that fastened with a pink clip, along with polished nails and fresh-from-Ulta makeup. Marny was only three years younger than Peach, but she looked so much more vibrant.

"What happened to me, Marn? I feel so blah."

"It's the menopause girl, but it ain't the end of the world. I'm serious about the spa day. We should go. I can't help you with the railing, though. Talk to Doug."

"My life isn't going to be fixed by a makeover. As for Doug," Peach rolled her eyes and shook her head.

"Come on, I'll buy you a latte and a chocolate croissant." Marny gave a little jerk of her head towards the door and they went inside, ordered their drinks, then took them to the comfy nook by the bay window that looked out on Main Street. Marny set down her bag of croissants and sipped her drink. She pushed a mug of chai latte over to Peach, dug the croissants out and set one in front of each of them on Café Faraway's branded napkins.

"What's going on, doll?" She waited, brows up, expectant.

After a few moments, Peach sipped her drink, set it back down, and picked at the corner of her croissant. "I'm having a weird day. My books came in and that was exciting, but …"

Marny's eyes got big and she let out a squeal.

"What! Oh my god, did you bring one?"

Peach continued. "… but! A bunch of them were ruined because Doug sat them in water for like two weeks."

Marny's brow furrowed over dark brown eyes and she plunked down her drink and crossed her arms. "Excuse me, what!"

Peach could see Marny was pissed and that Doug might lose a finger—or worse—so she tried to smooth it over.

"It was an accident. He didn't mean to."

"Didn't mean to my ass!" Marny's face only got more creased and severe.

Peach looked down and nodded a couple of times.

"Ok, look, I love that you want to kill him for me, but I'm already upset and what I need right now is for you to tell me all the reasons I should just skip this Romanticon thing. I've only got eighteen books for my table, which isn't very many. And it's my first book, and everybody else there will have a backlist, and more experience and …"

Marny tilted her head and interrupted. "What's a backlist?"

"All the other books they've written, of which I have zero. I just have this one. And it's probably not very good."

"It's good. I read it, remember?" She wiggled her eyebrows as she picked her drink back up and peered at Peach over her mug.

"You love me. You have to say that."

Marny's face softened for a moment, but she sat up straight and made a production of giving Peach an incensed look.

"Don't you remember that time you wrote a poem in sixth grade and I told you it was too sappy? And the time you picked that puke green prom gown with the high collar, and I steered you to a lovely aqua gown with a sweetheart neckline and Tommy Baliss ended up kissing you?"

Peach smiled as she accessed the memory, and then blushed. "We did more than kiss."

Marny's posture went conspiratorial, and she sipped and grinned. "You did not!"

"First orgasm."

Marny gave her a doubtful look.

"Well, with a boy."

"I'll be damned! Well, I love that for you." Marny slapped Peach's leg and her cheeks went pink. "Okay, Romanticon. How can I talk you out of something you don't plan on doing anyway?"

"I didn't say that," Peach explained, a bit sheepish. "I said talk me out of it. Clearly I'm thinking of doing it. I already have the registration approval … somewhere."

"Did you misplace that registration on purpose? You don't want to go, and you want me to confirm that's the right thing to do, yeah?" Marny raised an eyebrow, already knowing her assessment was one hundred percent correct.

Peach let out a sigh and nodded. "Yeah. Why am I like this?"

"Because you've been doing for everybody else for years and you don't think you deserve things. Did you call Tara to ask her opinion? I know she'll probably tell you to go, too. She should be here right now! I'm going to text her." Marny picked up her phone and started to text.

"Don't bother. Tara's been hard to get hold of lately. She's got half a dozen new hobbies since Kelsey left for college."

Marny screwed up her face and set her phone down. "What? I just saw her two days ago. She was asking about you."

"She was? She missed lunch with me last week because she got those face injections. Said she hated her elevens."

"Oh yeah, she did do that. She looks peaceful as fuck. Personally I cannot with the cow poison."

"I feel bad, she's so self-conscious. And honestly, I get it!"

Marny nodded in agreement. "Me too. Aging isn't allowed, especially for women."

Peach sipped at her chai latte halfheartedly. "I do miss

her though. You weren't there for our little pool party at the beginning of the summer. We ate wine popsicles and I laughed so hard I peed in my bathing suit. Let her have her injections."

"I'm not judging her, I just can't do it myself. No needles thanks! Okay, okay. If you don't want to go to Romanticon maybe you just need another year to feel ready. I'm not going to push you to do something that's just going to be awkward and traumatizing. But I really do think your book is good. Can I please see it?"

"I left them all at home. It felt weird to carry one around. Like I really believed I was an author or something. Kind of low-key bragging or tempting fate for somebody to laugh if they saw it sticking out of my bag."

Marny gulped down the rest of her latte and stood up, shouldering her handbag and putting out her hand for her friend to take. "I'm not going to push you to go to Romanticon right now, but I am going to explode if I don't get a signed copy of Peach Kincaid's first romance novel, so let's go."

Peach slumped in her seat and made a frowny face. "Really?"

"Yes, really. Come on."

Peach let Marny pull her up, then they hopped in their cars and headed to the solidly middle-class cul-de-sac where Peach's house sat with its two-story brick facade and beige vinyl siding and the rows of red rose bushes that Peach thought dressed up the area below the porch railing. As she got out of her weathered silver sedan she noticed that Doug's car was sitting in the garage.

Marny pulled in behind and got out of her sky-blue VW Beetle and noticed Peach was making a face.

"Ugh. I can't do this with him here. He's supposed to be

at karate! Let's just go back to the coffee shop and we'll do this some other time. Seriously, it's not even a big deal."

"The hell it's not a big deal! Okay, look, we'll just run in and grab the book and head down to Shrimpy's and have a cocktail and half a dozen different shrimp apps. We'll do it in a quiet little corner. I won't embarrass you, I promise." With her right index finger Marny crossed an X over her heart and made a pleading expression with her eyes.

Peach allowed herself another big breath and looked into her friend's pleading eyes, her resolve wavering.

"Pretty please?" Marny tilted her head and gave a big toothy smile.

Finally Peach said, "I'm sorry Marn, I'm just not up to it. But soon. I have to build up the nerve."

Marny deflated and put a hand on her friend's arm, "I understand. See you tomorrow maybe?"

"I think I'm going to have a wine slushie and read some Ramble. I'll call you if I come out of this well of self-pity I seem to have climbed down into."

"I'm going to text you on Saturday if I don't hear from you and see about setting up that spa appointment. Getting your hair and nails done can give you a whole new outlook. I know that sounds superficial, but it always cheers me up."

They hugged and Marny watched her friend of thirty-nine years meander up the sidewalk, reach out and touch a rose bloom, then go into the house. Marny turned on her little pink kitten heels and headed back to her car.

Peach went in the unlocked front door and saw Doug's karate clothes on the dining room table, tossed over some of her eighteen unblemished books. She didn't even have it in her to feel disrespected. She supposed she was like the proverbial frog in the boiling water; she'd been sitting in it so long she didn't even realize how cooked she was. She scooped up the clothing—careful not to knock any of her books onto the floor, though she didn't suppose it would have made much difference if she did—and headed down the avocado green carpeted hallway to the laundry closet. She put her hand on the knob to yank open the folding door but heard a squeak before she even had the chance to pull it. She realized the sound couldn't have come from the door, it was from down the hallway. She heard it again. Curious, she dropped the clothes on the floor and crept down to the end of the hall where the master bedroom door was cracked open a couple of inches and then she heard the squeak again, this time accompanied by somebody saying, "Oh Doug!"

She pushed open the door to find Tara kneeling on all fours on Peach's marital bed, her ass hanging over the edge, and Doug in his white track socks with yellow stripes standing behind her, pushing into Tara in a way Peach was sure he'd never done with her, even though she would have liked it. He always said he wasn't a dog and he wasn't going to do it doggie style. Her mouth agape she stood there while the two of them bounced and grunted and moaned. She was too stunned to process what was happening, like all of her emotions were shaken up and bubbling behind a cork. Then the cork popped and she threw the door all the way open, the knob punching into the drywall and sticking there. She heard her own voice saying "You have got to be kidding me!" but the "me" was more like "meeeeeeee" and it got louder at the end, punctuated with a red face and a bit of spittle as she bent forward and sort of vomited the word out of her body.

When she straightened back up again Tara gasped and was up on her knees, clasping one of the sheets over her naked body. Peach's sheets. Her 600-thread count, Egyptian cotton sheets with beige and gray dots that she had bought two anniversaries ago when her youngest moved out. Doug stood there, his cock hanging wet and limp, sticking to his pale hairy leg, his face sagging and his curls pasted down onto his forehead. His socks made him look ridiculous. Peach couldn't help but notice that Tara's face had that placid, recently injected lack of expression as her hands clutched the bedding and her chest heaved as she caught her breath.

Then Peach giggled. First it was a small giggle, and she tried to swallow it, but then she started to laugh. They looked so stupid, so caught. Before she knew it she was laughing so hard she was howling and backing away from the bedroom door while Doug reached over and plucked his ugly blue and red robe from a nearby hook. It was the last thing she saw before she grabbed a tote, tossed in her purse, her phone and one of her books, and bolted to the front door.

She had never been so glad to see that Marny was still in the habit of sitting in her car for fifteen minutes texting and scrolling social media before she drove away. Peach ran to the car, red-faced, tear-streaked, and laughing her ass off. She slapped the window until Marny unlocked the door and she jumped in.

"Take me to Shrimpy's now!"

Marny, though startled, didn't hesitate. She put it in gear and they tore down the street like Thelma and Louise.

Shrimp and Margaritas

Marny instinctively didn't ask any questions, even after they arrived. Instead she requested the largest booth available from the glassy-eyed, unsmiling twenty-year-old at the hostess stand. Clearly they didn't schedule their most sparkling staff for a slow Tuesday, but she did get the table right. Eight people could have been seated around the big corner they were escorted to—a perfect spot to huddle and talk. Peach and Marny entered from opposite ends and slid and scooted around the booth until they were right next to each other. Finally Marny looked straight at Peach and asked the question that had been boiling inside her the whole way over.

"What the hell happened, Peachy?"

Peach put her arm on the table and laid her head on it in a gesture of resignation.

"I know why Tara hasn't been talking to me," she said into the crook of her elbow. Then she sat up and a few tears rolled down her round cheeks, tracing her marionette lines and dripping off her chin onto the red vinyl table cover.

Marny stayed silent a long few beats, assessing her friend

while trying to put two and two together. Finally she said, "Margarita and apps first?" and Peach nodded. Marny waved over the server, who fortunately seemed to be several notches above the hostess in energy as he hustled right over. He smiled beneath slicked, perfectly black hair and pulled a pen from his apron.

"Hi, I'm Jackson. What can I get you ladies?" He took in the pair and quickly concluded that the first woman was a cheerer-upper and the second a cheeree.

"We'll start with two Cadillac margaritas, Jackson." Marny ordered. "No, scratch that, bring us two shots of whatever your best tequila is, *then* two Cadillac margaritas. Also, the shrimp scampi skewers, the stuffed butterfly shrimp, shrimp toast points, shrimp and artichoke cheese dip—really, just bring all your appetizers. One of every-thing. Please."

"You got it, ma'am," Jackson nodded, and took off towards the kitchen to drop off the ticket and then talk to the bartender. Marny looked back to Peach, who was clearly in need of a tissue. She fished one out of her purse.

"Now sweetie, what on earth is going on?"

Peach dabbed at her eyes and blew her nose, a little loud for being in a restaurant, which would normally have embarrassed the hell out of her, but she was past the point of caring.

"I just caught Tara and Doug … you know … in flagrante delicto," she sniffed.

Marny's eyes bugged out and she tilted her head like a quizzical cocker spaniel.

"Excuse me, what?"

"They were … you know … *doing* it. In our bedroom. My bedroom! On my anniversary sheets!" She was whisper-shouting, and felt all her emotions welling up in her throat again, like she might pop.

"Just now? When you went in the house?"

"Yes! Yes! Just now. They were in my bedroom." A few sobs escaped and Peach's chin quivered as she tried to get it under control. At least it was pretty dark in the corner, and thank god Marny was with her. Normally she would have called Tara with any big Doug news, seeking her pearls of wisdom about what makes happy marriages, and being her best self, and positivity attracting positivity, and all that other apparent bullshit.

"Now don't get mad, okay? But you're sure? Maybe they were just talking? Maybe she came to see you and he let her in?"

"Oh, he let her in all right. His dick was buried all the way in while she was on all fours. On my Egyptian … cotton … sheets!" Now she really started to cry, tears streaming down while sobs wracked her body. "He … still … had … his goddam socks on!"

The tissue demolished, Marny handed her the cloth napkin from the table as Jackson arrived with their tequila shots and two thoughtful glasses of water. He made eye contact with Marny and nodded sympathetically while she mouthed "Thank you." She picked up one of the shots and wrapped Peach's fingers around the glass.

"Here, let's do this, girl."

They both knocked back what was the best tequila Peach had ever had. She set the shot glass down with a satisfying thump, just as the margaritas and the shrimp dip with warm focaccia squares showed up. Peach felt too upset to eat, but the tequila needed a food chaser and that shrimp dip was the best in town. So she indulged. She still cried a little as she dipped her focaccia and sipped her margarita, while more shrimp bites arrived. Pretty soon she was feeling well enough to cry less and maybe talk a little more. Marny reached out and petted Peach's forearm, then gave it a friendly squeeze.

"Can I please see your book? Looks like maybe there is a new book by Peach Kincaid, hiding in your tote there?"

Peach sniffed and tugged out her book from her "Bookish Babe for Life" bag and sheepishly set it on the table upside down, at first keeping her hands over it and not letting go. Marny gently pulled her hands away and turned over the book.

Her face lit up and her nose crinkled with excitement. "Damn girl, this is fire!"

Peach cast a doubtful pout but Marny's enthusiasm would not be denied.

"I mean it! This model is so gorgeous, and these colors look great. I especially like that your name is nice and big. You deserve for your name to be nice and big."

"That's Ryan Slate. He's been on lots of romance covers. He's one of my favorites. Rose Ramble and L.K. Blake use him all the time." Peach seemed to be, if not quite cheerful, at least less morose. The food was helping. "This stock photo was older, like ten years old, so I was able to get it a bit cheaper. I know it's been used on many other covers but not with that shirt and tie."

"How does that work?"

"I hired Melissa's roommate Rebecca to fix it up. She's an art graphics major and she was able to alter the stock photo enough to make it look fresher. Made his haircut more modern, let him have a little chest hair, stuff like that."

"Oh, the hairy chest is back then?" Marny asked.

"I don't know, that's what she said. I like them smooth, and I like them hairy, I'm not picky!" Her eyes cheered up ever so slightly. "Anyway, I hired an editor from my virtual writer's group I joined during the pandemic, and Melissa's roommate made the cover. I wrote the blurb, which is not fun at all. And the SelfPubIt website helped me do the rest."

Marny's eyebrows went up, impressed, and she flipped the book over to read the blurb. Reading with various approving sounds, she finally said, "Darlin' this is so good. Just know that, okay? Don't doubt yourself. Hell, if you were a man, it could be half as good as this and he'd be crowing from the rooftops."

This time Peach actually laughed, and then heard herself laugh and felt a little weird about it. But the magic of tequila and shrimp was working.

"Can we have one more margarita, Marn? And now I'm in the mood for some chocolate mousse cake. Want to split a piece?"

"Absolutely!" Marny quickly spotted their server. "Jackson! Let us eat cake!" she called out. The young man scuttled over to take their dessert order and gathered up some of the plates and glasses before heading towards the kitchen. Peach poked a stray shrimp around on her plate.

"Thirty-two years, and just like that. Dynamited! Blown up! Done." Peach inhaled deeply and let out a long audible sigh. "What am I gonna do Marn?"

Jackson appeared with the margaritas and cake—one plate, two forks—and took away the rest of the empties. Marny lifted up her glass and tipped her head forward, encouraging Peach to do the same.

"I think you're going to go to Rambling Romanticon, that's what. Cheers!" And she clinked her glass to Peach's. Even though Peach hesitated for a moment, she sat up straighter, nodded, and took a long sip of margarita. Then she sunk her fork into the tip of the chocolate mousse cake.

FOUR

Absofuckinglutely

By the time Peach got home, Doug, chicken shit that he was, had already packed a bag and left a note on the kitchen counter.

Dear Peach,

I wanted to tell you. Tara wanted to tell you. We just didn't think you'd understand. You know things haven't been great since the kids moved out. Like, you stopped cooking my favorites, you didn't want to go see any movies I wanted to see. All the things I liked you didn't care about. When you told me you never even liked football, it was like everything in our marriage was fake. You and me just don't work anymore.

Tara loves football, she loves making me dinner on karate night, she really cares about the things that make me happy. We just fit better.

*I'm staying at Lenny's for now. We can talk after
you've calmed down. It's not fair to make me feel bad
about wanting some happiness and passion in my life.
I deserve that, and you should find some happiness
too.
—Doug*

Peach narrowed her eyes at the letter as she read it a
second time, then crumpled it up and threw it down on the
mustard yellow and walnut brown vinyl flooring. The
margaritas a distant memory, she yanked open the freezer,
pulled out a merlot popsicle and held it in her mouth as she
peeled off every stitch of clothing. Her round dimpled
bottom and jiggling thighs walked right out of the sliding
glass patio door and down the steps to the shallow end of
their in-ground pool, where she waded in until her middle-
aged breasts were floating. Peach leaned back, licking her
popsicle and watching the stars appear as the sky got darker,
until she finally felt ready for a shower and sleep.

Later, wrapped in a towel, she headed for Melissa's old
room, now half filled with crochet supplies, and flopped
across her single bed, trying not to think about the noises
she had heard down the hall earlier. Once the sandman
finally found her, she slept like the dead.

PEACH WOKE to her phone alarm chirping on the bed. She
was disoriented for a moment, tangled in a pink bath sheet
and surrounded by lavender wallpaper and baskets of yarn,
until everything came flooding back. Even so, she didn't get

as upset as she might have expected, because for the first time in she couldn't remember how long she didn't have to get up and make Doug his coffee. She didn't have to make sure he had clean underwear or that his Little Debbie snacks were stocked in the pantry, so he could grab one before he padded down the hall to the spare room he had long ago claimed as his office. She had thought the absence of him would make her sad in many ways, but she only felt one thing: relieved.

Moments later the phone blared again, this time buzzing a familiar trill. It was Marny calling, and as she sat up Peach found her head was throbbing a little. She flopped back down and put Marny on speaker.

"Hello … your buzzing is too loud."

"Good morning sunshine. My client rescheduled their house viewing this morning so I booked us a full spa day. So get your butt up, drink some water, and take some ibuprofen, I'm picking you up in an hour. And don't worry, I'll have your mocha latte with me. Don't even try to beg off." And the line went dead.

Peach didn't really feel like doing anything but clichéd relationship-on-the-rocks stuff like eating ice cream washed down with whiskey and lying on the couch watching sad movies for weeks. Maybe they were clichés for a reason—it felt like the thing to do at this moment. But trying to stop Marny on a mission was like trying to stop a designer bulldozer, and Peach had to admit that she really had a way of making things seem so much less awful than they might actually be. She gathered her resolve, rolled out of bed, and gave herself a quick rinse down and shave, just in case anybody was going to be seeing her naked at the spa.

At 9 a.m. Peach was standing on the front porch in a big orange tee that had at least three holes in it, a pair of boxy cotton shorts, and a giant pair of sunglasses, her hair in a messy topknot of pale brown and gray. She pulled a cheap lip balm out of her pocket, smoothed the waxy stuff over her lips, then stuffed it back in her shorts as Marny drove up with a beep-beep that went right through Peach's temples. She winced and walked down to the little blue Beetle and got in.

"This car is too small for my curves. Damn belt is always acting like it's not going to reach."

"It reaches, you're just tired and hungover. Here." Marny pulled some extra slack and helped her click the belt into place.

"Why do you always look like you're about to get your photo taken?" Peach lowered her sunglasses to take in Marny's classy-casual outfit. "Even in a tee and jeans you look so put together. What the fuck?"

Marny smiled. "It's the diamond stud earrings, they shine up any outfit." She clucked at Peach. "Oh my goodness, we need to get some breakfast in you, and we're getting our massages first. Here, take your coffee."

Peach melted a little with gratitude. "Oh my god thank you so much you are a goddess walking the earth!"

"So I've been told." Marny peeled out down the little suburban street and opened the moon roof.

Peach sipped the sweet chocolatey coffee concoction and closed her eyes, letting the breeze relax her. She didn't think of Doug the whole way to the spa and once there, she was determined to let those spa minions have their way with her.

This wasn't Dolly's Day Spa, the one she normally went to just off of Main Street. No siree, Bridle Creek Resort & Salon was once a horse ranch, but the big house and outbuildings had been converted to luxury spa facilities. Peach and Marny started with sauna and massages, then went for full facials, until they were glowing, dewy and oily, and smelled amazing. Peach almost felt, dare she say, relaxed.

"Let's get you a manicure and pedicure for the convention. It'll make you feel more polished, more professional. You are going aren't you?"

Peach considered it a moment and for the first time that day she thought of Doug, off doing whatever the hell he wanted. He always did whatever the hell he wanted. She thought of Tara, Miss Positivity and Manifestation, manifesting Peach's husband. And then she thought of how good and right it felt to write that book.

"Yeah, I'm going. Can we cut my hair too?"

Marny lit up like a Christmas tree. "Absofuckinglutely! Let's get you the works."

Peach furrowed her brow. "I don't need the works, just a touch up."

"Consider it a celebration present for getting your book published. Let me do this, sweetie, please?"

Peach relented, and soon found herself in the upscale salon in the big house, choosing a manicure style.

"French tips, short and almond, please."

Half an hour later she was admiring her new nails while Steph the stylist fastened a leopard print cape around her neck.

"What kind of cut do we want?" she inquired. "And are we going to do something with this gray? Or just do a shine treatment?"

Marny looked at Peach, who shrugged.

"You're the makeover artist here, Marn. I'm just going along for the ride."

"Alrighty. Shoulder-length, layered, side-bangs—yes, yes, I know they aren't on trend, but they look amazing on her.

Dye it dark brown with cherry red lowlights and leave the silver streak."

It seemed Marny had been thinking about this for some time. Peach hesitated only a moment, then nodded her assent.

"Let's do it!"

FIVE

Departure and Arrival

"You know, only the very best friends drive you to the airport," Marny said with a big grin as she tossed Peach's carry-on bag in the back seat.

"Oh, I know. You are the very best," Peach teased. "And thanks again for that spa day. I do feel pretty damn good, though I'm not sure I can pull off this hairdo."

"What, are you kidding? You look fantastic. And with the black tips? Adds a little edginess. It's more like the you I remember. The you that's still in there. How do those jeans feel?"

"Pretty good actually. Clearly I haven't been shopping in forever. Who knew how much curvy fashion was out there these days? It was just too easy to do sweats, I guess. Wasn't like Doug appreciated it when I went out of my way to get something I felt cute in. Or sexy in. He didn't care a bit."

"I'm sorry, babe. That sucks. But, you've got an awesome weekend ahead of you and you are *not* gonna miss that flight, so let's go."

Peach had been able to fit her books into her luggage by splitting them up a bit and putting a few copies in her carry-on. She still felt a little hot flash of excitement every time she saw the book cover and ran her fingers over it. Or maybe that was just menopause. She was pretty sure it was the excitement.

She had forgotten how thrilling travel and adventure could feel. She'd been a homebody, a caretaker, a put-everybody-else-firster for so long that it surprised her how easily she was able to tap into her essential adventure-girl self now that Doug had fucked around and slunk off. Which ultimately meant that she could do more for herself now—and that she should assure herself that she was allowed to do things she liked to do, things that were just for her.

Still, flying was never easy for Peach, so she was glad Marny walked her nervous ass as far as she was allowed to go, and waved her a heartfelt bon voyage. It wasn't until she sat in her seat and the plane started to taxi that the real nervousness kicked in. An anxiety attack was trying to take root, so Peach did her best to breathe through it, eventually popping on headphones and watching the in-flight movie, which happened to be *My Big Fat Greek Wedding*. She was glad now that Doug had refused to take her to see it, so she could enjoy it without that baggage.

She did pretty well on the two-part flight, and was even feeling a little victorious. That is, until they reached the gate and everyone unbuckled and began standing up. Peach reached up to get her overhead luggage, and her jittery stomach caused her to pass gas. Not too loudly, but loud enough that passengers nearby—including a young hippie couple who looked like an ad for Burning Man and an attractive well-dressed man in a suit and a purple fedora— witnessed the toot. She wanted to melt down and trickle away under the seats. She wanted to walk into the ocean. Move to the moon. It was as if the whole bubble of people around her paused for a moment. The gorgeous hippie couple whispered a little and exchanged some suppressed grins, but it seemed maybe nobody else noticed. Peach guessed she'd never see any of them ever again, which was the only thing that kept her from lying down in front of the plane's wheels.

"Not off to a good start, Peach," she said under her breath.

She collected her luggage, got in her RideShare and headed to the convention center, which was thankfully a good half hour from everybody and everything to do with that airplane. At least she was less nervous now that she was back on solid ground, and she did like the new jeans, sensible-but-sexy sandals, and the low-cut blouse she was wearing, so she was able to regain something akin to confidence.

She still wasn't used to the super short hair, but it did have a certain sass she was settling into. The black tips made it kind of cool, and she didn't mind the stripe of gray either. Almost looked intentional. It wasn't that she suddenly appeared ten years younger, as she had before, but she felt like she was carrying her age a little better, which improved her outlook by a couple of notches at least. So maybe she wasn't a real author quite yet, but she could look the part. She assured herself that the incident on the plane was not some sort of harbinger for what was to come over the weekend.

SIX

Is That Really a Meet Cute, Though?

The driver dropped her off at the hotel, which was tall and shiny and unlike any she'd ever stayed at, not even when she and Doug went to Chicago for that fancy wedding a few years back. Just inside the three-story lobby were signs for the Rambling Romanticon, with Rose Ramble's photo larger than life, wearing her signature red suit and lipstick with a rose tucked behind one ear. One of the posters was at least ten feet tall and it listed off all the attending authors' names, in alphabetical order. That was when Peach saw her own name positioned right in the middle of the list. Her heart skipped a beat. Seeing herself on that oversized roster both excited and terrified her, and she started running over in her head all the things she'd brought and worrying about things she might have forgotten.

Peach was almost afraid to go up to the front desk. Other people were filtering around her, many of them looking like real authors wheeling their crates of books and tabling supplies. Most of them looked polished, cool even, and she was glad she had taken an antacid while she was waiting for her luggage an hour ago—there would be no repeats of what she would forever think of as The Plane Incident. But what was she doing there? She wasn't a real writer, except technically you could call her one because she'd written a book. But does one book really make you an author? And she was self-published—does that even count?

Peach still squirmed a little whenever somebody mentioned she was an author. Her whole life she'd only been "girl" or "wife" or "mom." And really, it was the pandemic that got her started, when she was so depressed with the world she needed a place to escape. That place turned out to be the basement, in the corner with the only window and an old desk she'd found on the curb. She hadn't written anything since college. She never did get her degree. It was the same story a lot of women have—she got pregnant, and home and family became her priority. Her dream of writing stories was replaced with dreams for her children.

So she camped out in the basement while the world burned around her and she wrote a sexy love story. She pounded out a hundred thousand words, emerging only for wine and snacks. Then found herself an editor and a cover designer and published it.

Peach reminded herself that none of those questions about identity mattered. She was here, and she was going to see it through. She took a determined breath and began the long walk to the counter with her wheeled luggage in tow, forcing one heavy foot in front of the other. She spotted the fresh-faced twenty-something desk clerk, open and ready for her next guest. Peach was one stride away, her goal in sight, when a blur in a red designer suit cut in front of her, trailing a cloud of hairspray and expensive perfume. Peach's eyes opened wide as the woman rested her Louis Vuitton bag next to her shiny red pumps, held up an ID badge, and with glossy red lips said, "Rose Ramble, I believe I have a suite for the Romanticon. The rest of my luggage is over there." She pointed with a long red-lacquered fingernail to her right. "Don't scratch it, please." The signature rose in her hair seemed to be observing the scene from atop Ramble's head.

The clerk put on a practiced smile and called for an attendant, and with a few clicks of the keyboard and a swipe of the room key printer, the woman in red was handed her keycards and instructions to her room.

Ms. Ramble thanked the desk and strutted past the throng towards the elevator, leaving guests agape in her wake and not even looking back as the lanky attendant stacked her four large bags onto a trolley and scurried to keep up with her clicking stilettos. As he rolled the cart past the clerk he shot her a pained look, and she returned one of sympathy, her lips pressed tight, the corners of her mouth downturned. As soon as she noticed Peach hovering quietly, she snapped back into her customer service role with a brisk and proper, "Welcome to Chesapeake Towers Resort and Convention Center, how can I help you?"

"Hi. Um, I, well I'm one of the—I'm here for the Romanticon," Peach sputtered.

"Are you an author or attendee?"

"Well, an author, I guess."

"We just need your ID and the card you reserved the room with."

"Oh yeah, of course." Peach dug awkwardly in the new bag Marny had gifted her on their makeover shopping spree. It wasn't designer, but it was nice, though she wasn't used to it yet. Nothing was where she thought it would be, and she regretted that she'd merely turned the old bag upside down into this new one and didn't take time to organize it. After unzipping and checking several pockets before finally finding her wallet, she looked up to see the man in the purple fedora from the plane and they locked eyes. His look was a knowing one, unless she was imagining it. And at that moment her searching hand yanked the little chain on her wallet, flipping the purse and sending everything from that compartment skittering across the hard white and black marble floor, with a clatter that seemed to echo endlessly across the entire lobby. Peach's face went hot as she scanned the renegade items, hoping none of them were too personal, and noticed the line of well-heeled women and men waiting at the counter, watching her with more than a little side-eye —though Purple Fedora at least gave her a sympathetic downward grin.

"I'm so sorry, I'm nearly done," she apologized to the entire line as she squatted and began scooping up lip gloss, several quarters and dimes, some chewed gum wrapped in a scrap of newspaper, a linty sourball, and a pillbox that thankfully had not popped open.

It was then she noticed a large pair of well-worn motor-cycle boots near her, and looked up a long leg of denim that led to a black tee and a flannel shirt on the most attractive forty-something man Peach had ever been within ten feet of. He squatted down wordlessly and began helping her gather her items. She thought to herself with some horror that this was usually the part of the story where the attractive man would find a condom, pasties, a tampon, or maybe a bottle of Xanax, and she offered a quick prayer that none of her things were that embarrassing. Fortunately for Peach, all he held in his large hands were an orphaned hoop earring, a bobby pin, and two pennies.

"There ya go," he said, standing again and smiling at her. She stood too, and at full height only came up to his chest. Peach looked up at his dark hair, slightly silver at the temples and salt and pepper everywhere else, and she froze, mouth open, as the light flooding in through the floor-to-ceiling windows surrounded him with an angelic glow. He lifted his hands a little higher.

"Did you want these?" Her things looked so tiny in his enormous hands.

She snapped awake, her soul coming back into her body, and she held out her bag with the middle pocket open wide for him. He tipped his hands and in they tumbled.

Peach cleared her throat as she looked up at this man she could only imagine was some kind of dreamy lumberjack.

"Um, thank you."

"Of course, ma'am," he winked and she watched a moment as he walked away.

Ma'am? Ouch. But the wink? Did she imagine that too? Probably an involuntary tick.

"Excuse me," she said in a small voice. He didn't hear her so she said it louder. "Excuse me!"

He turned to her and raised his brows.

"Yes?"

"Do I know you? You look so familiar." She tilted her head.

"Oh, sorry." He returned and extended a hand. "If you're here for the convention, you might have seen me on a book cover sometime. I'm Ryan Slate."

Peach's jaw went slack and she looked at his hand as if it weren't real. She reached out gingerly to take it, realized her mouth was hanging open and shut it. It took a few moments before she could speak again.

"Yes, actually, I do know you. I mean who you are. I

mean I can't believe I didn't notice, I've seen your … Well, I'm Peach Kincaid."

Ryan smiled wide, showing two rows of gorgeous white teeth, and the corners of his eyes made a lovely crinkle. "Nice to meet you Peach. It happens all the time. You'd probably have recognized me if my shirt was open."

Peach looked confused.

"You know, because of the romance covers." He smiled again. "See you around," he said in a smooth baritone that made the back of Peach's neck tingle.

She let go of his hand as he backed up a couple of steps, but they held each other's eyes for a moment. Then he was off to grab his bag. She was feeling rather lightheaded when she heard some mumbling behind her and turned to see a flurry of pens clicking, notepads flipping, and mobile devices being thumbed as every author in line appeared to be taking notes.

Blinking, she turned slowly back to the clerk. "Camille," her tag read. Camille gave her a sympathetic and curious look, took Peach's ID cards, and in seconds she had her room key and directions in hand. Peach headed towards the elevator like she was floating on a cloud, though with one wheel on her luggage now squeaking and locking up. With a huff Peach hoisted the bag and hurried to the elevator, which soon opened and thankfully was empty. On the ride to her floor she could see her reflection in the shiny walls and noticed she was blushing. And the color in her cheeks made her feel pretty.

Her room was on the eighth floor, which meant she had a nice view of the Chesapeake Bay. There was a little gift bag on the bed with a thank you note from the event organizers and Rose Ramble herself, who was the major sponsor. Peach kept reading "Welcome Author" over and over, hoping it would feel right if she read it enough times. Nah, still didn't feel right. But she figured as long as she was there, she would pretend it was.

She texted Marny.

> I'm here. Room's nice. Look at this nice note that was in a little gift bag. It says I'm an author.

Peach snapped the image and sent it. Marny texted right back.

> That's because you ARE an author! Enjoy this. You deserve it.

Peach dug in the bag and discovered some cosmetics, a mini bottle of whiskey, a bottle of cola, a small rose shaped box that contained four chocolates, and an advanced copy of *Know When to Hold 'Em*, Rose Ramble's first book in a new cowboy series. Peach gasped when she saw it and opened it —it was signed by the legend herself.

She unpacked her new clothes and a few of her favorite older pieces and hung them all carefully, slid the two pairs of shoes she'd brought into the closet, and assessed her tabling stuff. She used the little writing desk in her room to practice her set-up. Since she couldn't bring a lot of stuff with her, she'd made sure what she had was easy to pack and looked on-brand, though she wasn't too sure what her brand looked like yet.

She spread out her black tablecloth and laid the hot pink "Peach Kincaid Romance" table runner over it, displaying her name on the front of the table. Shit! It was printed a little crooked—she hadn't noticed that before. She scooted it a bit to make the words more straight, but then the bottom of the runner was on a slant.

"Ugh, I give up," she muttered.

She left it crooked and took out three folding plate stands, setting a copy of *Greyson Edging* in each one, then stacked the remaining fifteen books up next to them.

She also set out the little sign she'd made for scanning a QR code to buy the ebook. That was Marny's idea, and it made Peach feel like she seemed more techie than she really was. It never would have occurred to her to use a QR code. Melissa whipped up the sign in no time on her laptop and sent it to a local print and copy shop, where Peach went over and picked it up—all in one day. Amazing. It wasn't fancy, just her name and an old headshot photo from a community play she had been in nine years before. One of the few pictures of her she actually liked. It had the book colors of gray, black, and pink, so it all tied in nicely.

Peach slid the sign into a clear plastic stand, and voilá. Nothing all that special, but it would do. She stood back and looked at the whole thing. Pretty plain display, kind of pathetic compared to what others would have, but she couldn't really do anything about that now.

There was supposed to be an author soirée this evening but she was pretty sure she wasn't going to attend. She had brought a dress—a brand new black and pink one-shoulder gown that hugged her curves like you wouldn't believe. Marny insisted she buy it. The pink cut across her chest and the black satin nipped in just a little at the waist while hugging her curvy bottom and thighs, then flared out again at the hem. It gave her almost a mermaid shape, and she'd never had a dress quite like it.

Oh well. Another time, mermaid dress, she thought.

But honestly, she did feel a lot fancier with her new

hairdo and acrylic nails. Marny even loaned her some black diamond dangling earrings. It'd been so long since she'd worn any, Peach was surprised her earring holes hadn't closed up, but when she tried them on they looked perfect with the dress. She pulled it back out of the closet now and hung it on the curtain rod so she could admire it, even if she probably wasn't going to wear it.

She kicked off her sandals, tugged off her stylish new ass-hugging jeans and low-cut shirt, and tossed herself onto the bed. She was by herself at a classy hotel, with a gorgeous dress, her book that she wrote, and had face-to-face encounters with Rose Ramble and Ryan Slate. Ryan Fucking Slate! She hadn't expected him to be graying. Somehow he had seemed eternally on the verge of thirty.

She threw herself giddily onto the bed, extracted the chocolate box from her gift bag, and popped the rose top off for a look at them. She gave the box a sniff, and dropped one of the little rose shapes into her mouth. The snap of the coating was lovely and inside was, of course, rose crème. Rose creams! That woman was a marketing genius, and absolutely committed to concept. Peach pulled out the little whiskey bottle and drank it down sip by sip. She sighed, leaned back onto a stack of lovely fresh pillows and stared at her gorgeous new dress while she ate another chocolate. *Is this real life?* she wondered. Then she remembered her cheating husband, her airplane embarrassment, and that she wasn't really a writer.

"Well, I won't tell anyone if you don't, li'l friend," she mumbled conspiratorially to the empty whiskey mini.

She snapped a selfie of popping a chocolate into her mouth and sent it to Marny, who told her she needed an Instagram account or some such. Peach was never much for social media. But then again, she hadn't been particularly social anytime in the past, oh, thirty years, unless it was with other PTA moms or the wives of Doug's coworkers. From time to time she did attend a cast party or two, and those were lots of fun, although her community theatre days had always been curtailed by needing to take care of her domestic duties.

Now though, she could take care of Peach. She could do the things Peach wanted to do. She could put Peach first sometimes. And maybe she would just go to that soirée and show off her new dress and haircut and nails after all.

SEVEN

The Full Romanticon Gala Experience

Peach had a hard time zipping up that gown by herself—something she hadn't anticipated as an issue when Marny was helping her into it and telling her how spectacular it looked on her. With some serious hunching and pretzeling though, she managed.

Next she slid on the black sparkling sandals she'd gotten because they were sexy and not too high. For Peach, the eternal hunt for sandals that were wide enough while also being sexy and low-heeled was something akin to spotting a unicorn. Though she was fairly short at just five-four, she was never comfortable in heels. She knew plenty of women who could wear stilettos with the swagger and confidence of a runway model, but for her it would mean twenty minutes of fun followed by the total distraction of her aching feet for the rest of the night. Or her infamous clumsiness would strike and she'd trip over a shadow or something, right in front of everybody. But these dressy sandals were definitely in the unicorn class. Her bright pink toenail polish peeked out from the straps, and Peach was feeling pretty damn fine, if she must say so.

She took some more antacid, drank a big glass of water, and dropped her lipstick, powder compact, room key, cash, ID, phone, and breath mints into a black satin clutch and stood back to look at herself in the room's floor length mirror.

"You got this," she said, and waved a little at her reflection with her newly manicured nails. She ran a hand over her hair to smooth it, turning her head this way and that, watching how it would swing and bounce. Then she caught sight of her wedding ring set—the one that Doug had helped her pick out on their tenth anniversary because they could finally afford something a little bigger in the diamond department. She'd loved that ring at the time, and for years after, but now it felt like a lie. She reached to pull it off, hesitated a moment, then yanked it free and tossed it into her jewelry pouch. Peach turned on her short, glittery heels and headed out the door with her head held high.

She attempted to strut to the elevator, but with her short legs and tight dress it came off as more of a confident toddle. No matter. She pressed the button and ten seconds later the elevator opened, packed with people dressed to the nines, and she sent a mental thank-you note to Marny for talking her out of the business casual route.

"Room for me?" she piped up without a moment's hesitation. A tall, lanky young woman in an emerald satin pantsuit waved her in.

"Room right here."

Peach had never relished trying to stuff herself into spaces—she felt self-conscious about taking up too much room and "bothering people." But in this moment, she claimed her space and scooched into the elevator with a friendly wiggle of her eyebrows as the doors closed behind her.

When they all filtered out toward the first floor ballroom, Peach exited with the tall woman and looked up at her.

"Thanks so much," she said warmly.

The woman revealed a large toothy smile under her hawkish nose.

"Oh of course. Love your dress, by the way."

Peach looked down at her gown as though she had no idea what she was wearing and said, "Oh, this old thing?" and they both laughed.

"I'm Peach." She extended her hand to the woman.

"I'm Laura. Are you an author? I know this soirée is supposed to mostly be authors, but I know some other publishing folks are here too, including some editors and, oh …" she leaned down closer to Peach's ear as if she had a secret, "and some of the models. That's always fun." Laura straightened back up, her dangling rhinestone earrings winking in the light.

As weird as it still felt, Peach said, "Yes, I'm an author. I've only written one book though. And I'm self-published, so …"

Laura held her hand up to stop her midstream.

"Little helper words here, okay Peach?"

Peach studied her and waited.

"When somebody asks you if you're an author, just say 'Yes.' If they ask about your book, you should have ready a quick little way to tell them about it. Leave the rest unsaid. No need. Okay?"

"Um. Yes, okay." She was suddenly feeling embarrassed and the confidence she'd had just moments ago retreated back to the eighth floor. It must have shown on her face because Laura leaned in again with a conciliatory expression.

"You'll get the hang of it. You've published a book. You made it into this event, and they're kinda choosey. Especially with just one book. So just keep that in your pocket, okay?"

Peach nodded but started to wonder again just how she did make it into this event with all these more seasoned authors. She leaned in towards Laura.

"I think they let me in by mistake," she said in a low voice.

Laura took a long breath and studied Peach.

"Peach, that's one hell of a lucky mistake then. You make the most of it."

"Noted," Peach replied. It hadn't occurred to her to think of it that way.

"Since you're new you're going to feel all weird walking around the ballroom looking for where you should sit. It's like you're the new kid at school wandering around with your lunch tray. It sucks, I know, so if you want, you can sit with me."

As they approached the doors to the ballroom there was a large standing backdrop with the logos and names of the largest sponsors, and a photographer was taking pictures of people posing in front of it. Laura and Peach paused for one quick shot there and then entered the ballroom.

It was like a crazy, over-the-top, soft-focus romance author dream. The tablecloths were black satin with red velvet runners, while the centerpieces were glass books tucked with long stem roses. There were little red foil favor boxes at each seat and rose petals spread around every table. A large red satin banner was behind the table where the DJ was set up, and all around the dance floor were several large stand-up signs with images and names of the cover models in attendance—five men and three women. And standing next to each sign was the model.

Peach's heart skipped three beats. Laura looked at her and smiled.

"I know, right?"

"Right," was all that Peach could manage. After another beat she said, "Laura?"

"Yeah?"

Peach looked up into her face.

"I don't mind telling you, I feel out of my depth here."

Laura put a hand on Peach's shoulder.

"Let's go find us a seat."

She followed Laura to a table near the right edge of the dance floor, which happened to be two stand-ups away from Ryan Slate. Tonight he was wearing a sharp charcoal suit with a black and gray striped tie over a striped gray dress shirt. The suit was tight and showed more than suits usually do, and Peach had to keep looking past the drop-dead gorgeous women models standing closer to her table to sneak peeks at him.

Rationally, she knew a model was never going to be interested in her, especially one as popular and devastating as Ryan Slate. Not that she was looking, of course—she was still a married woman, even if that marriage was in big trouble. But oh boy, that man was inspiring Peach with some romance story ideas right now, and if nothing else came of this weekend, at least she had that! She was going to type the hell out of some new scenarios when she got home. They were stories that would probably never see the light of day though, as she had already concluded this was her first and last foray into the author world.

The two women were the first to the table, but soon three others were there, each greeting Laura like a friend and giving Peach a nod, at which point Laura would introduce her. Peach was excited to meet them all, and one of them was an author she'd actually read, which she was glad for because she couldn't escape this feeling that she should have read at least one book by every author in the room, even though she knew that would be no easy feat. She picked up the program lying in front of her on the table and quietly looked up their names in the list to make mental notes, then had the bright idea to take a peek inside the red foil box. There she found a beautiful red pen, much nicer than your usual giveaways, and began putting little checkmarks next to the names of the people she'd met.

Laura tried multiple times to pry her from her seat to introduce her to others beyond the table, but Peach was feeling like she'd used up all her adventure allowance. Then the DJ started playing line dancing songs, and Laura tried again to cajole her out of her seat.

"I'm not good at those. It's been too long," she begged off—although she did slide her way to the bar twice and each time asked the bartender to "give me something pink." She also stopped by the apps table and grabbed some tiny meatballs, some crackers and cheese, and chocolate covered strawberries, which she imagined wouldn't be easy to eat politely, but she was going to try anyway. Both times she had her fresh pink drink in front of her, Laura slid into the chair next to hers and they took a selfie together, which apparently she was posting on Instagram. Then she would take a video of Peach with her pink drink which she said she would also post on TikTok. Peach was sure it was the first video of her ever on TikTok. Lots of new adventures this week.

The other authors at the table were circulating, dancing and drinking freely. They would lean in together and laugh, making all manner of faces depending on their various levels of tipsy. Nearby, the models would pose with each other when asked in front of black velvet drapes apparently provided for this purpose, and they also circulated throughout the room. She watched some of the braver people—or just more tipsy—as they danced on the floor, and most of them were not good. But they were having fun, and that was all that mattered. Laura was pretty good though, and one other woman in an aqua tulle princess gown. As for the rest, it was like watching highschoolers, something Peach knew a lot about, having chaperoned every high school dance that her kids Lydia, Jack and Melissa had gone to.

She had just picked up the chocolate covered strawberry and was examining it when she felt a hand on her bare shoulder and heard a voice in her ear.

"Well hello there, good to see you again."

She turned her head to see Ryan Slate's face just inches from hers. *Ryan Fucking Slate!* Her first thought was that she was very glad she hadn't said that out loud, followed by the realization that the wink she thought she saw earlier might have not been her imagination after all. But it was still ridiculous—this guy could have any woman in this room. Why would he be interested in her?

Talk, Peach, talk!

"Hi."

Eloquent, Peach. Say something else! Be clever! Be funny! All she could think of was that it was a good thing the last thing she ate was grapes and not cheese. R.F.S. rounded her chair and sat in the seat next to her.

"Would you like the full Romanticon Gala experience?"

Again, the tingles running down her spine. *How does he do that, just with his voice?* She noticed too his smile was a little crooked. Adorable. But the math wasn't adding up—he was at least ten years older than the other models in the room, but easily ten years younger than Peach. Still, she very much wanted to know what this full gala experience was about. She wrinkled up her recently shaped brows ever so slightly, confident that they looked nice at least.

"I think I probably should, don't you?" She couldn't believe she was actually trying to flirt with Ryan Slate, but by now she was too wrapped up in the moment to feel dumb or awkward about it.

"May I?" He looked down at the strawberry in her hand then back into her eyes.

"Oh, sure … here," she said, and handed it to him, not really knowing where this was going. Should she have offered it, for some reason? But she'd already had her hands all over it—like, ew, germs. Why would he want that?

He took the green leafy end between his fingers and gently brought the strawberry tip to her lips. She was trying not to get flustered, but the vibe he was giving off was so sensuous and the drinks made her feel a little heady. *This is it, girl. Which way do you jump?* Throwing caution to the wind she bit into the berry, her eyes locked with his, until she closed them and finished off the sweet chocolaty bite. She swallowed and opened her eyes again and thought she must be in some fever dream or magic mirror. This couldn't actually be happening, not to her. It could have happened to twenty-year-old Peach, maybe, but not fifty-two-year-old Peach. Not soft-bodied, dimpled, gray-haired Peach.

"Good, right?" he asked.

"Yes, good." She gave him only a close-lipped smile, aware that she might have chocolate on her teeth. She took a sip of the melted ice water at the bottom of her glass and ran her tongue discreetly across her teeth. "So they pay you to feed the ladies strawberries at these things?"

He smiled bigger this time, and ate the other half of the strawberry.

"Nope."

He wiped his hands on the napkin in front of her, his eyes on her eyes the whole time, then winked and walked away leaving her speechless, her heart beating ten times faster than it was a moment before. She felt parts of her go flush with blood and her smile turned from cautious to something more venturesome.

Laura slid into the seat where Ryan had been and gave Peach's arm a squeeze.

"Oh my god, are you kidding me?"

"What?" Peach pretended to be mystified as to what she could be referring to.

"Peach, you had a meet cute with Ryan this morning, and now he comes over here and chats you up? Come on—spill!"

Peach waved off Laura's observation.

"A meet cute?" She chuckled. "This isn't a romance novel, Laura. I mean, Jesus, if you had any idea what has happened to me this week, and then on the blessed plane—never mind, forget I said that—anyway, you would not be thinking I'm living a real-life romance novel." She punctuated the thought with another laugh and a raspberry at the end. But then the lightbulb came on.

"Wait, you saw that this morning. Shit, a bunch of people here saw that this morning. Me going gaga over Ryan Slate." Peach sank down in her seat, not even thinking about the line of her dress any more.

"Well, maybe some of your week sucked, but it looks like your weekend is going okay. Me, I'd ride that, um … wave, if I were you."

Peach narrowed her eyes. "Do you think that he was intentionally flirting with me? Earlier, I mean. I swear I saw him wink."

Laura nodded. "I do."

"But I am a middle-aged empty-nester from the suburbs. I don't exactly give off sex goddess vibes." Peach paused in thought and then tilted her head. "Do I?"

"All I know is, that man is flirting with you and you look great tonight." She slapped the table. "I'm getting another drink and I'm going to do the Electric Slide—it's coming up, I checked. Then I need to call it a night. Tabling check-in is 9 a.m."

"Have fun, wild woman," Peach said with a smile as Laura rose. "And Laura …"

Laura paused and looked over her green satin shoulder.

"Yeah?"

"Thanks."

"Welcome. See you tomorrow over the coffee pot." She swung her long red hair back around and it bounced as she shuffled away.

Peach could see Ryan circulating around the room, and it seemed to her he wasn't getting too close to anybody other than for photos—not like he did with her, when he fed her that strawberry. Maybe she was reading too much into it, but Peach liked the way this idea felt, even if she didn't much trust it. She gathered up her new pen and a little to-go plate of meatballs, stuffed mushrooms and a few pink petit fours and headed up to her room to wind down. The last thing she saw as she stepped from the raucous ballroom into the all but silent hallway was a petite blonde dragging Ryan to the velvet curtain for a photo.

She made the lonely sojourn back to the eighth floor, her eyes following the gold ribbon pattern down the hallway carpeting. She let herself into her room and peeled her dress off, carefully hanging it back up. It smelled of the evening—

booze, food, and her peach vanilla body spray—but it still looked great, with the exception of some lap wrinkles.

She washed her face and slipped on her PJs, which was really just a big Stevie Nicks tee and a pair of soft stretchy black underpants that Marny called "hip huggers." Aptly named, they did show off her butt rather nicely, if she did say so herself.

She settled into the giant fluffy bed and turned on the TV, tuning it to that lovely British baking show under the tent and leaving the volume low. She wasn't entirely sure why, but it always seemed to have a calming effect for her. She set her phone alarm and nestled down into a pile of pillows that she didn't have to share with Doug. Or anybody. For a moment she felt a stab in the chest at the thought of all the years they had been together and how he could just lie to her like that. Right to her face. And Tara. She lost two of the major people in her life in that one moment. But with all the new things that had happened in the last few days, she was able to push those tormenting thoughts aside. She watched the people making the best pies and cookies they could while talking in their British accents, until she dozed off with a smile on her face.

EIGHT

A Peach Out of Water

Peach woke with a start, realizing there was sunlight streaming in the window but she hadn't heard her alarm yet. She hated that feeling of being late for something important, and her stomach, which was already on thin ice, immediately turned into a knot to go along with her mild headache.

She rolled over to squint at her phone—8:19 a.m. Shit. What the hell was going on? She knew she'd set her alarm, and opened her phone to check it. 7:30 p.m.

Ugh! Peach!

She hopped out of bed like her ass was on fire, rushed to the shower and took a quick one, dried her hair and threw on her makeup, all in record time—especially considering her hair and makeup routines were both new. Thankfully she already had her outfit picked out: a bright pink silk satin blouse with a dramatic lapel and a dreamy drape, diamond stud earrings—classic, as Marny would say—and a pair of black wide-leg slacks, which Marny swore were all the rage right now. Peach wasn't too sure about them at first but they actually looked pretty good, and they were comfortable, so bonus points. And with her low black pointy pumps, she thought the whole outfit looked pretty sharp.

She dug down into the gift bag for her badge and slid it over her head, turning the tag up to read it.

PEACH KINCAID
Attending Author

Again she felt that rush of excitement that made her heart speed up a bit. She turned to look in the mirror and almost didn't recognize herself, which maybe was a good thing. She could pretend to be "Peach Kincaid, Author," instead of just plain old Peach, crafter, mom, and wife, and nobody here would be the wiser.

She put her books and table display items into her rolling suitcase and walked out into the hallway, which was abuzz with activity. She had to wait through two elevator cycles before she could get downstairs, which made it a couple of minutes after 9:00 when she finally got to check in. Fortunately it didn't seem like a big deal, as there were lines at the tables and no one would even know she was late. She allowed herself to breathe a sigh of relief and get into her Peach Kincaid, Author headspace. She'd smile. She'd talk to people. She'd give her business card out. It would be great.

She was waved in by event staff and given a map to her table. When she couldn't find it she was led there by a nice young woman in a headset and all black clothing. Her tag read "Eryn, Event Manager" and Peach felt like she was being such a bother, but Eryn was gracious and professional as she dropped her off at her table, then immediately headed off to put out another fire that had come in over her headset, calm but moving quickly.

The ballroom they had been in last night looked completely different. Peach's table was sandwiched between two authors she'd heard of but hadn't read yet. Their displays were large and lush and they both had stickers and pens and pop-up banners that stood six feet tall. Peach felt kind of like a kid with her little display and no swag, and she was kicking herself for not at least getting some stickers. She did her best with the empty table space, spreading her cards around, artfully tilting them this way and that. At least she was proud of the card, with the same colors and photo as her sign, and she felt like she looked pretty good in the outfit she was wearing. Marny was right. Dressing up, doing your hair and nails and all of that, really could have an impact on your confidence. Or in this case, it was kind of like wearing a costume that she could hide inside and be something or someone else for a bit.

Peach only needed a few minutes to set up her lean table, while other authors had so much stuff to put out and put up, they had personal assistants helping them. With nothing else to do she sat down behind her table and started looking up the authors next to her online so she'd at least know what to talk to them about. Turned out both wrote historical romance with mild spice, but she was only a couple of minutes into the search when Laura stopped by her table.

"Hey, Peach," she said, peppy and chipper and not, apparently, hungover in the slightest. Ah, the benefits of youth. Today Laura wore an all-orange pantsuit with a nipped short jacket that made her look like she had a mile of torso, which she kind of did. She also had an orange headband in her red hair, which was in a low bun this time instead of loose and flowing like last night. Her only color besides the orange were the pink swirls on her orange crepe blouse and her pink ballet flats. Peach imagined that Laura wore a lot of flat shoes so she didn't tower even higher over everybody.

Peach tucked her phone in her back pocket and stood up with her friendliest smile.

"I love your orange outfit, Laura! Where's your table?"

"Oh, I'm over … there." She pointed across the ballroom to the farthest corner.

"That's a bit of a jog."

"Yeah, it's a good spot though, so I'm happy with it." She looked at Peach's table. "So, are you … all set up?" she asked with as much diplomacy as she could muster.

Peach wrinkled her nose. "Yes, unfortunately."

"Oh."

"Yeah, it's a long story." Peach straightened a book that wasn't crooked and looked sheepish.

"Y' know what? It's fine. Don't even stress about it. Think of it as a learning moment." Laura held up a finger. "Next time though, swag."

Peach was thinking there wouldn't be a next time. She was doing this so she could say she did it and not die regretting that she didn't do it, plus get Marny off her back, *plus* forget about that shitshow with Doug and Tara for the weekend. This was her first con, and it would be the last, and thinking of it that way made her glad she'd only ordered two cases of books, two tablecloths, one box of business cards, and no swag.

But rather than get into all that she simply said, "Definitely. Swag next time. Can I see yours? You know, for ideas?" Not that she actually needed swag ideas, but she very much wanted an excuse to not sit there behind her meager display while everybody else was still setting up.

Laura lit up. "Of course! Follow me."

Peach walked behind her past half of the ballroom's other tables, and pretty much all of them were loaded and well displayed. Laura's setup was just as nice as everybody else's, boasting little book racks, stands, a six-foot poster with a recent headshot of Laura in a green fedora, eyes sparkling, lips coated in glossy pink. Most of her materials were green, orange, and pink, and she wrote what appeared to be erotica and contemporary sweet romance. Her banner read "Laura Langcroft, Sweet & Spicy Romance for Every Taste." She had stickers, magnets, little lapel buttons, bookmarks, and ink pens, all coordinated and on-brand. Peach sighed inside.

Laura swept out her long arms. "What do you think?"

"Wow, I freaking love it!" Peach enthused. She kept saying to herself that she wasn't jealous of Laura at all—she was too nice to be jealous of. But Peach couldn't help nursing a wee bit of envy, and felt even more out of place than before.

"This here is a culmination of seven years of work and about thirty book events large and small that I've been to. When I first started I only had twelve copies of my book and a white tablecloth I got at Target. It takes time. It's gonna feel like everybody is so far ahead of you. Just keep going." She gave Peach a sympathetic look and patted her shoulder. "You look great. Very professional vibe. Very authorly."

Peach could feel herself blush.

"I still think they made a mistake."

"Well, like I said, enjoy the mistake, you're lucky they did."

Peach nodded, not feeling especially lucky, but making the effort to shift her perspective.

"I guess I should get back to my table. Things are supposed to get going in about fifteen minutes I think."

Peach pressed her lips together and gave an awkward thumbs-up, to which Laura chuckled and waved her off.

"You'll do fine. Just be sure to talk to people. Know how to describe your book!"

Peach nodded and waved over her shoulder as she walked past table after table of authors fine-tuning their displays. Despite her resolve about never doing this again, she couldn't help making mental notes about the things they had—bowls of candy, drink koozies, clever mugs, printed totes. She did a double-take when she saw an erotica author's table laden with tiny penis keychains. "Have a peen!" the author was saying. Peach didn't think penis keychains were in her future. She didn't think any swag was in her future! All the same, when she got back to her seat she pulled out the mini-notebook from her gift bag and jotted down some of the more interesting items. Then she drew a little word balloon to the side that said, "This is a dumb list because you aren't an author and this will never be your life." Then she shoved the notebook deep into her purse and put her author persona back on and smiled at everybody that smiled at her.

If anybody thought her display was pathetic, they didn't show it. And as the event carried on Peach was pleasantly surprised at how nice all of the other authors were. Well, most of them. One woman was kind of snippy when Peach asked her about what swag she favored. "Why don't you just Google where to get swag?" was her retort, as if Peach was going to steal her ideas. And one of the few men there cornered her during the lunch break to tell her what he thought her next book should be about. She felt a little singled out by this, as though this guy saw through her paper-thin disguise, until she realized he seemed to have plenty of unsolicited advice for the more established women authors as well. Well, the joke was on him, there wouldn't be another book anyway. But everybody else she talked to was supportive and full of helpful ideas and information. Maybe they just didn't see her as any kind of competition—that made total sense.

There were reader attendees rolling by with carts full of books, clearly there to get as many things signed as they could. Others carried bulging totes, while some had slimmer bags, and Peach imagined they were on tighter budgets, but they had more time to talk with the authors, including her. Finally, around 3:00, just a couple of hours before the end of the event, she made her first sale to a dark-haired young woman sporting a large "eye-heart-rose" button. Peach had practiced at home using the swipe device that plugged into her phone, so when she slid the card through everything worked just fine. The young woman asked her to sign it, and Peach took out her new Rambling Romanticon pen. Even though she felt a little silly, this was her first real signing, and it made her unexpectedly proud.

"Make it out to Ashley, please. A-s-h-l-e-y."

Peach wrote the brief inscription without shaking, which in her mind was a major accomplishment.

"There you go. Sorry, I don't have any bags."

Ashley smiled. "That's okay, it's going right into my tote with some friends."

"Thank you Ashley, enjoy." Peach wasn't sure what else to say, so she stood silently as Ashley gave a small wave.

"I'm sure I will," she said, and walked to the next table.

Making that sale seemed to burst some kind of dam, because Peach then sold six more books, signing each one, and two people even used the QR code to order e-books, which she couldn't wait to tell Melissa and Marny about. Nine books, in one day. Peach couldn't believe it. It made her feel like a million bucks. Then she wondered if that was lame, with other authors nearby selling fifty or more.

Her last customer was a young woman who could not have been more than twenty in a tight bubblegum pink tee with "Book Slut" in rhinestones stretched across her ample bosom and a perfect sheet of shiny black hair parted in the middle. She mentioned her name was "Kinzie with an i-e," and she wrapped her long, pointy, elaborately decorated nails around the cover and said, "Oh, zaddy." Peach had never heard that term before, but she got the gist.

Then Kinzie with an i-e said, "I buy everything with Ryan Slate on the cover. I like this old pose, it's a classic. Been Photoshopped a bit to age him up, but I'd know that jawline anywhere."

Peach was stunned for a moment, not realizing people bought books just for the models on the cover. Not a lot of people, probably, but she supposed it made sense for the models to have a following too.

"He didn't mention this book on his socials, though."

"I don't think Mr. Slate knows he's on the cover. In fact I know he doesn't know. This is an old stock photo I bought, and I'm not with a regular publisher. It's just … well …"

The girl studied Peach with the distant coolness only a twenty-year-old can summon.

"Right. Well, I'll take it anyway," she said finally, and even though she sounded a little judgy, Peach was doing a happy dance inside while she signed the book to K-i-n-z-i-e, and waved as she walked away.

By about thirty seconds after 5:00, most of the authors were already half packed. They seemed to have it down to a science. She pulled her suitcase out from under the table and loaded the ten remaining books back into her bag. She noticed she wasn't the only one packing up unsold books, so she didn't feel too much like a failure. Some of the other authors were grumbling a little to each other, but most of them were happy and upbeat, if a bit worn out.

Peach had everything stowed away in less than ten minutes and headed for the ballroom doors along with everybody else. She wasn't sure, after being "on" all day, if she would have any energy left for the after-party. She knew Laura would probably be there. And, to tell the truth, she wouldn't mind a little more harmless, ego-boosting flirting with Ryan either. She knew it was silly. He was paid to be nice to the ladies. She herself paid about $1600 for this weekend, between the plane, the hotel, and the vendor fees, all to sell about $125 worth of books. And that wasn't even counting her new clothes, hair, and makeup. So why not enjoy the act? She could pretend a bit longer that she was an actual author, and that a hunky romance cover model wanted to flirt with her.

As she bravely plunged into the crammed-full elevator, with its dizzying bouquet of perfume, cologne, rayon, and sweat, she felt like she'd accomplished something kind of important. To her, at least.

She arrived at her hotel door with a contented sigh. Even if she didn't go to the after-party, at least she'd done okay today as Peach Kincaid, Author. And tomorrow some of the bigger authors with long backlists were going to teach workshops and sit in on panels, and Peach fully intended to take advantage of everything she paid for. This would be her best chance to do anything like this, so what could it hurt?

NINE

The After Party

Peach slipped out of her slightly wilted blouse and headed to the bathroom. The first thing she noticed was that she should have touched up her make-up after lunch. Her lipstick was all worn out in the middle, leaving a fuzzy pink line rimming her contours. Her foundation too was looking less than fresh. That was the thing with aging skin, it took so much work to look "naturally" dewy and hydrated. She hadn't paid much attention to "old" women when she was young, and never imagined how much work it could take just to feel like you were presentable. It's easy to throw on anything and look good when you're twenty. Makeup, no makeup—doesn't matter when you have fresh, lovely young skin to start with. *Oh, the things we take for granted,* she thought to herself.

For the most part, Peach had been fairly content living in her stretchy pants and well-worn tees, her no-makeup days and TV nights. Thinking of it now brought a pang. Nachos and beer and zombie movies on Friday nights was something she had actually enjoyed with Doug. Now that the stress of the day had melted away, she found herself feeling kind of sentimental about her marriage. She unconsciously rubbed her finger with her thumb, the way she sometimes did to straighten out her wedding ring, and remembered it wasn't there.

It was true that she had faked some things with Doug, about liking things he liked, and not just football. She did that, she admitted, so he would want to spend time with her. And because she loved him and wanted him to be happy doing the things he liked. But she also did it so he wouldn't cheat on her. She'd been told over and over since she was about eight years old that men who were catered to were less likely to stray. She understood now that that was a load of crap, but how was Doug to know what she'd been taught since she was eight? She could be better with him, she was sure, now that she had proven something to herself. Now that she felt more like her own person.

She pulled out her phone and went to Doug's Facebook page. He posted even less frequently than she did, and she figured the most recent item would probably be from five or six months ago. But no. In the past year he'd posted at least twenty times, and pretty much every week lately, which utterly shocked her. Maybe if she'd been online more, she'd have noticed.

Going back to last year he posted about things she didn't even realize he was aware of, like the pandas leaving the National Zoo, a new brewery in downtown Pittsburgh, and an article about glassblowing being a dying art, as well as two posts about Steelers games he'd gone to, and various holiday wishes for people, including Mother's Day, Easter, Thanksgiving, Christmas, and New Year's. Here and there were a few photos of yellow roses without any text, and birthday wishes to the kids that Peach herself had posted with photos of the family and Doug tagged in.

She scrolled back up to the top and saw that just today Doug had changed his profile picture from the photo of the two of them on a cruise to the Bahamas a few years back to one of him by himself. She squinted because he looked a little different. She clicked it and noticed he had a fresh haircut and, oh my gravy, he dyed his gray! He was wearing a Steelers jersey she hadn't seen before. She'd bought and laundered every shirt he owned over the last thirty-two years, but not this one. She felt a little queasy.

Peach clicked over to his photos tab and scrolled through all of the images, and one from his karate dojo caught her eye. She clicked and it filled the screen. His karate instructor had posted it two and a half years ago and tagged Doug and the rest of the class, and then she saw it. Tara, right next to Doug. Dammit, how long had this been going on? It might not mean anything. Maybe they were just innocently taking karate together. But she had a feeling down in the pit of her stomach that that was where it all began, and that Tara had given him the Steelers jersey. She clicked on the link for Tara's profile, which was loaded with football stuff, little "you probably won't share this" posts, videos of kittens, and various photos from karate. She clicked through them and Doug was in every one. She also had a bunch of yellow roses in a vase as her cover image, posted the same day Doug last posted a photo of yellow roses.

Her face got hot. She navigated back, or meant to, but instead she accidentally liked one of the karate photos that they both were tagged in. She immediately unliked it, but the damage was done; they would both be getting a notif-ication, and Peach knew all she could do was leave the coun-try. "Ugghhh!" she raged through a tightened mouth. She threw away the Facebook app and tossed the phone to the floor.

Unable to sit still with her bottled up anxiety, she paced a few turns around the room, her mind whirling. The only plan of action she could come up with was to finish getting out of her clothes and put on her PJs and see if Room Service had any Ben & Jerry's on hand. But just as she felt the hot tears welling in her throat, she caught sight of the slinky black tank dress waiting quietly on the hanger. It was an awesome little number, and she had really been looking forward to wearing it. With the shiny red belt and red peep-toe slingbacks Marny had paired it with, the whole ensemble gave off peak Pat Benatar vibes.

"Fuck all y'all," she said out loud to Doug, Tara, and anyone else was trying to put her in a corner. She stomped into the bathroom, slicked her hair back, made her eyes smoky, and painted on red lips. First came the sheer black bra and control panty with lace insets—not exactly thong territory, but not in grandma country either. Then she pulled the sleek dress over her head, and remembered why it was a must-have. It had both stretch and weight to it, and it draped and clung in a very sexy way that begged for a shimmy. She slipped the belt around her waist, stepped into the red shoes, and pounced in front of the long mirror, trying various angles and striking a few poses.

"Hot damn! Look out, Ryan Fucking Slate!"

She quickly oiled up her legs and for that finishing touch, gave a little spritz of her signature scent under her neck, under her arms, and one up the dress for good measure.

She grabbed her author gift bag and dumped it out on the bed. Where were those drink tickets? She dug down inside and found them stuck under a seam—it was like Felix the Cat's magic bag of tricks in there. She headed toward the door and then remembered that authors were all invited to bring a copy of their book to the autograph table for everybody at the con to sign. She thought that would make a nice parting gift from her one weekend as an author, so she grabbed a copy of *Greyson Edging* from her suitcase and trekked down to the elevator with a fair amount of swagger. She knew she was over half an hour late, and she didn't care. Almost everybody was in the ballroom already, leaving the elevator and hallways all but empty.

Peach could hear the music thumping and saw colored lights bouncing all over the room through the doorway. She felt a little like Alice about to plunge down the rabbit hole as she crossed the threshold. A mirror ball threw coins of light across her body and the low roar of people talking was punctuated with laughter from every direction. Again, the transformation of the room from the tabling event a couple of hours ago to this romance writers' disco funland amazed her. She had to hand it to the event staff, they were good.

She went first to the bar and collected a glass of red wine, then she crept around the edge of the room looking for the autograph table to leave her book on. It didn't take long to spot it, and there were at least thirty books lying there already. There was a sign asking everybody to sign them, so she sipped wine and signed books, taking in the covers, the colors, the various styles and brands. She kept her autograph smallish and tucked it into corners. It looked like a lot of signatures had already happened, so she hoped her book wasn't too late to get some too.

Peach turned around and saw Laura sitting near the edge of the dance floor again. This time she had on a blue satin pantsuit and a feather and net fascinator secured alongside her red French knot. She looked over and saw Peach making her way towards her and waved.

"Nice fishnet gloves," Peach said.

"Smokin' hot dress!" Laura said.

"Mutual admiration society," Peach said, and they both laughed.

"Are you having fun?" Laura asked.

"I only just got here. Dropped my book on the signing table. Would you please sign it?"

"Of course I will! I wouldn't miss out on being a keepsake in your first of many book conventions."

Peach's laugh was small, but she was no longer preoccupied by the idea that she wouldn't be doing this anymore. She was ready to wear her author persona again. And who knows what the future might hold?

"Are you going to be here for the workshops and panels tomorrow?" Peach asked.

"Hell yes! I wouldn't miss it. I'm telling you these ladies know what's up. Try and get into Cassie Lair's workshop about plotting. Oh, and the one about imposter syndrome. That woman changed my life. Trust me."

Peach nodded and smiled. "Okay, I'll be seeing you there."

"Lover boy is over there chatting up the sexy volunteers. Did you see him?"

Peach looked over and her heart sank a bit. Which was kind of dumb since she barely knew the guy, and she was still married, and ten years older than him, and didn't look like a model. But she couldn't help feeling that crestfallen ache in the middle of her chest when she saw a volunteer adorably batting her eyes at Ryan.

"Oh, Ryan? I wasn't looking for him," she looked back at Laura, who was having none of it.

"You were too. Go over and talk to him."

"Maybe in a while. I'm going to go grab another drink. Might as well get the freebies out of the way."

The DJ put on "Cha Cha Slide" and Laura screamed and shot up towards the dance floor.

"Okay, bye," Peach said to herself.

She hit the bar and this time asked for a shot of rum with a cocktail chaser—a Southern Comfort double with peach schnapps and a cherry. It was a drink she came up with for her fortieth birthday, and she had named it "Peach's Cherry." That was when she was into community theatre, after Lydia and Jack were out of high school and little Melissa was old enough to sit quietly in rehearsals for a few hours and do homework.

That birthday party was the best she'd ever had. It had a pirate theme and great decorations thanks to her theatre friends, and the costumes were fun and sexy. Even Doug looked dashing in his puffy shirt and pirate hat. He rarely cut much of a figure, but Peach had never held that against him. She herself felt sexy that night wearing a little waist cincher and a stripy short skirt with a low-cut ruffle blouse.

That party was also the first time she'd ever kissed a woman—the date of Doug's work friend Karl. Tina was her name, and she and Peach had gotten lightly toasted on a couple of Peach's Cherries. All night they had been chatting about the many things they had in common—favorite movies, places they both wanted to travel, even singing the Heart song "Magic Man" together—and it was after everybody had sung "Happy Birthday" to Peach that Tina threw her arms around her and gave her the kind of kiss she'd only ever gotten from boys. She didn't hate it, honestly, but it was kind of embarrassing since it was in front of all of Doug's coworkers and Tina was only about twenty-five. Still, Peach didn't stop until Tina was ready to stop. When the kissing was over her she'd looked in Peach's eyes and said, "Girl, you are juicy."

She never saw Tina again, and never asked about her. But she and Doug fucked like bunnies all that week because it turned him on so much. Best birthday week ever. The next time she saw Karl, he was with somebody named Kimberly.

Peach took her Peach's Cherry and walked over to a table in a corner not far from the book table, where she'd spotted a couple of undisturbed favors and place settings and figured those seats were fair game. The centerpieces from last night had been recycled, now accompanied by six or seven tealights and dinner tapers that made them glow at the base and the top. Instead of a red foil box with a pen inside, there were red foil chocolate hearts scattered everywhere and tiny keychain replicas of some of Rose Ramble's book titles, which made Peach very happy.

She took a sip of her cocktail and looked around the room. The Cha Cha was over and they had moved on to Def Leppard, and most of the folks were still grinding it out on the dance floor. Peach wanted to dance. She loved to shake it down a little, but she already felt so looked-at this weekend, she couldn't do it. Another sip, and she leaned her head back to savor it, which was when she saw a commotion out of the corner of her eye over at the book table. The models, including Ryan, had all swarmed it, checking out the various covers and talking animatedly, holding books up and showing them to the others, then signing them. She figured they were finding the covers they were on to autograph. Then she remembered her book had Ryan on it and she tried to slide down in her seat and hide behind the flower arrangement in case he looked in her direction. And as soon as she imagined that, he did, almost like he had heard her thoughts. She leaned farther, trying to obscure his view of her, but it was too late. He was already walking over with something in his hand.

Please don't let that be my book! Please don't let that be my book! Please don't let that be my book!

"Peach? Hey, Peach, is that you?"

She gave up, took a deep breath and sighed it out. She sat up straight and waved a quick wave, taking another sip of her drink as Ryan cleared the centerpiece and came fully into view.

"Hi, Ryan. You remembered my name."

"Of course I remembered your name. It's adorable, just like you." He flashed one of those lovely smiles of his. Disarming. He knew he was disarming. He did this to all the ladies, she was sure of it.

"Is this your book?" He held it up for her as if she couldn't possibly have guessed what he was holding. She pressed her lips together and nodded in tiny little nods and tried not to roll her eyes.

"Yup."

"Did you know this is me? It's an old shot, but it's me."

She continued nodding. "Yup," she said again. He tilted his head and looked at her.

"Hey, are you okay?"

She realized she must have looked like she was carved of wax, nodding like a bobblehead on the dashboard. She took another sip and closed her eyes for a second to focus on the warmth going through her. She told herself that she is an author and this is a great and lucky conversation she was having and she was not so nervous she was about to pee. The stakes couldn't be lower—all she had to do was eat party apps, get slightly tipsy, and go home tomorrow to the real world. She took another cleansing breath and smiled softly.

"I would love it if you would sign it, Ryan," she purred. It had been over thirty years since she flirted with a man.

She was pretty sure she was sucking at it, but she remembered she looked amazing in her dress and she had actually sold ten books today.

Ryan leaned over the table, and she watched him write. Tonight he was wearing dark jeans cuffed at the ankles, laced ankle boots, a pale plaid button-down shirt and a blazer. He looked like an ad for lumberjack dress clothes. Perfect. She got a whiff of his cologne, smoky and spicy, just like half the romance books she'd read. Perfect. So perfect in fact it only underscored how unreal all of this was.

"I'm going to go put it back on the table, but don't go anywhere."

She started to stand but sat back down and watched him walk to the book table about twenty feet away. They really were in a quieter corner of the party, near the side exit and the kitchen doors. She didn't mind, it let her feel less watched.

Ryan had turned around and was starting to walk back when Peach decided he needed to see her entire sexy ensemble, which would naturally inspire him to ask if they could take a photo together, but when she stood up she tipped over her untouched shot of rum. In a knee-jerk reaction she grabbed for it and instead knocked over one of the tapers onto the rum-soaked tablecloth which lit up like a brush fire in August. The whole center of the table was instantly in flames.

Peach let out a scream but before she could even move Ryan had grabbed the fire extinguisher by the kitchen and was running towards her. Why she didn't have the sense to stand back was a question she would ask herself for years after, but when Ryan let loose with the extinguisher, a lot of the thick white foam ended up all over Peach and her sexy outfit. Even her face didn't escape Ryan's spray, after he'd shot it all over her and the table.

The music suddenly stopped and the entire room went eerily quiet. Peach stood there, frozen, hands by her side with palms forward, looking stunned. Ryan was simultaneously assessing her for injury and watching for any remaining flame.

"Are you okay?" His voice had a definite note of concern. Peach just wanted to fall apart into her atomic components right there. She nodded slowly, and the room began to buzz again with quietly shocked comments. Ryan was very close to her now, offering himself for her to lean on.

"You're sure you're okay?"

Peach wiped a little foam from her lips.

"Other than being more embarrassed than I have ever been in my entire life, I think I'm okay. I'm kind of wishing though that I had gone up in smoke myself."

Laura had run over from the dance floor, breathless.

"Peach, oh my god! Are you okay?"

"Physically, yes. Can't say about the rest."

Peach chanced a casual look behind to see everybody in the entire ballroom facing her direction, and determinedly turned her head back toward the table. Laughter was rippling around the room now. She knew that under her foam, she was beet red from head to toe.

"I know how to help," Ryan said, and threw his jacket on the chair nearby. He crossed behind Peach and whispered, "Brace yourself."

Peaches eyes widened with concern and she tried to sneak a peek over her shoulder at what he was doing without catching a glimpse of the crowd. Then Ryan kicked her chair away, and she felt his arms around her—one behind her back and then, as he bent, one behind her thighs —and he scooped her up. She let out a surprised squeak and instinctively put her arms around his neck, which left them nose to nose, their faces only inches apart.

Ryan turned a little and paused, breathing heavily. Even his breath was delicious, and she could smell rosemary in his hair. He seemed to be surveying his options, or maybe he was just posing for the room, but then started taking long slow strides through the crowd. Peach looked only at Ryan's face as they moved past everybody, but she could tell they were clicking photos, shooting video, and taking notes, as any true romance writer would. Yes, she was mortified, but she was also warm and tingling every place Ryan was in contact with her. She caught sight of Laura trailing behind them, who smiled and gave her a thumbs up, and Peach, despite herself, smiled a wicked little grin back at her and tightened her grip around Ryan's powerful neck. She had an impulsive, nearly irresistible urge to lick him there.

Once they were through the ballroom doors, Ryan rounded the corner so they were out of sight. She was far more disappointed when he set her down than she would have expected. She heard the music start back up, and then the room exploded with applause, followed by laughter and loud conversation. Peach peeked through the hinge crack for a moment and then turned back to Ryan.

"Well you certainly know how to make an exit!" It wasn't anything close to what she really wanted to say, but this was how it went when she had no words but silence was even harder. "Wow, this stuff is sticky, and it doesn't really go with black I must say." Then she caught sight of herself in the mirrors across the hallway, and saw the damage wasn't as bad as she thought—only slightly mussed, if fully humiliated. She started laughing, and for a solid minute she couldn't stop, and every time she looked at Ryan's concerned expression she only laughed harder, until it wound down finally and she let the last of it out with a heavy sigh.

"Oh, Ryan. I feel so dumb. I stood up because, I thought, I would flirt with you one more time before I headed up to my room. And it's silly, but I was feeling like I looked pretty cute in this outfit and I wanted you to see it." She wiped away a little foam she felt tickling her shoulder. "Then I hit the candle," she said with a sweeping gesture, "and I know, I know, I'm being ridiculous. You, a model. Me, a middle-aged lady you never met before this weekend. And it's just so silly, but it kind of seemed like you were flirting with me, and I really, really liked the way that felt." She looked at him with tender eyes and put her hand on his perfect chin.

"I mean, if you were even *kind of* flirting, I'm sure it was because that's part of your job. And that's totally fine, I get it. It's like you have this super power of being flirty and gorgeous. But I haven't felt that way in so long it was so easy to get caught up in it."

She was dangerously close to kissing him, she could feel it deep down. She backed away a bit so she could talk more with her hands.

"See, I was pretending to be this author. I mean yes, I wrote a book, I'm not a liar. But I was feeling like a fake." She began to pace. "I just am not on the level everybody else here is, y' know? I don't do author things, I don't live an author life, even though I would like to be, *really* like to be, an author. I don't even know how I got in here, but I felt like if I pretended, maybe it would help me ..."

She trailed off to see if Ryan had anything to add to the

conversation, but he was just looking down at her with a soft sweet grin that reached the corners of his eyes.

Nope, too much quiet. She was going to go back to the kissing idea if one of them didn't start talking.

"Actually it did kind of help. You know, pretending. My friend Marny took me out to get this haircut and some new clothes so I could feel more confident and professional, because I did *not* look professional, Ryan … trust me on this. And I don't mean like IBM tech support professional, or lady district attorney professional. More like edgy artsy professional, y' know? Like a romance author—which duh, that really makes sense, and Marny does have a good sense of style and I trust her." She dared another look at Ryan's face.

"And then there was you, and you were so good at helping me pretend to have this wonderful exciting life …"

She trailed off again because Ryan had taken another step towards her and she felt a lump in her throat. He was looking in her eyes and she was steeling herself to look right back. She swallowed a little harder than she meant to and hoped the sound hadn't carried outside of her body as loud as it seemed inside.

He leaned in, closer. She didn't back away. He put a large hand on the soft curve of her upper arm—it was so warm she felt like it would leave a pink hand-shaped mark if he were to take it away. With his other hand he gently swept away a little foam from her cheek. His smile faded while his eyes penetrated her with such intensity it made heat creep up her torso, her neck, her face. Even her ears felt warm. He had a gravity that was pulling her ever closer.

Her head tilted up, her eyes stayed on his until she closed them, she put her hands on his chest, and their lips met. His mouth was soft and warm and tasted of wine and want. Their tongues did a slow soft dance for a few moments. Peach felt her warmest places pulsing. Then they parted. It took her a moment to open her eyes and look at him. She almost didn't want to open them at all, ever, but instead just hang there in that moment for as long as possible.

When she did open them he was looking at her with such a sweet happy expression, she couldn't help but return the energy herself. The thud of the bass behind her was low and slow and vibrated through her, her heart beating in time with it. For that moment she was thinking of nothing but desire and delight, while everything else had faded around to the edges of the world. He spoke first.

"Would you like me to take you to your room to help you clean that foam off?"

Peach very much wanted him to take her to her room and help her clean the foam off, but she couldn't say yes. She couldn't actually make any words at the moment. So she just nodded.

He took her hand in his—the warmth of it, the largeness of it exciting and new. They walked to the elevator and the doors opened. She pointed to eight. He pressed it. The doors closed and as the elevator rose, her tummy flopped inside and she wondered if she should pinch herself awake, or if she was a cheat no better than Doug. She looked at her reflection in the elevator and expected to see her own shame, but what she saw instead was this sweet, sexy hero standing next to her, holding her hand and looking down at her with warm affection, and she thought, *Peach, you deserve this.*

Once at her door though, she had a moment of hesitation. Was this a revenge fuck? Was it even going to be a fuck at all? Maybe he really was just going to wash the foam off of her, very sweetly, very helpfully. She stuck the key card in the slot, but instead of waiting for the green light, she turned to him.

"I really don't know if I would just be using you if we did this."

"Using me how?" He crossed his arms.

"I just caught my husband of over thirty years cheating on me three days ago."

"Ouch."

"With one of my best friends."

"*Double* ouch."

"Yeah. And I'm just thinking, I feel like an out-of-control teenager right now. Who knows what kind of weird feelings would come out of me if we … you know. It's embarrassing, but he's the only man I've been with since college. I'm sure you've been with a lot of, um, experienced women. Beautiful women."

His arms stayed crossed and he nodded.

"So what you're saying, Peach, is that you're emotionally vulnerable right now and you aren't sure this is what you want to do?"

Peach's eyes widened. *Damn, he speaks woman.*

"Well … yes, exactly."

"In that case, my lady, I bid you adieu." He took her hand and wiped it clean of foam and kissed it. He gave her a wink and a wicked half grin that she wanted to eat, and turned on his heel and strode away. Peach watched his fine form as he did.

"Peach, you're insane," she sighed to herself and pushed through the door. She immediately slipped off her shoes and belt and climbed into the shower in all of her clothes, washing the day away.

She knew it was the right choice. It would have been

classic rebound revenge sex, which often didn't end up feeling great. Or so she imagined—it's not like she had any personal experience with that. In fact she'd only slept with three other people besides Doug, and none of them were rebounds. She always needed a little recovery gap between boyfriends.

Once in her comfy Stevie Nicks tee, Peach pulled out her laptop, curled up on the bed and typed "Ryan Slate cover model" into the search bar. There wasn't a lot to read about. He had an Instagram that seemed to mostly be dedicated to his modeling career. She clicked on the reels tab and scrolled through. Many of them were little behind-the-scenes moments from cover shoots. A couple of him cooking chili or lasagna—likes to cook, that's a nice thing to have in a man. Not like she would ever have him as a man. That was just absolutely ridiculous.

When she clicked on the kitchen photos she realized he was cooking in a firehouse. She scrolled back further through his posts and found one of him in fireman's turnout gear hauling a hose. She assumed that it was another model shoot but when she read the caption it said "Just the usual drills with my volunteer firefighter fam." So he's a firefighter *and* a model. *This is unreal. You can't make this stuff up,* Peach thought. *Well, you can actually. Lots of folks who do are at this hotel right now, but that's beside the point.*

Nothing in the photo indicated where exactly he was a firefighter. She found a couple of posts on an old Facebook fan page that hadn't been updated in a couple of years. Probably due to the pandemic. But in 2019 there was a post of him at an animal shelter posing for a calendar with other romance cover models to raise money for the shelter. Okay, now this was too much.

She clicked back over to her own page with its gazillion

unread notifications, because she never was good at checking them. She had likes from her kids on various things like the birthday posts, a few photos of food and dinner recipes, a photo of Christmas cookies from last year—all with comments and likes. She read each one now, and liked them and responded with smiling emojis, some over a year late.

She had been fighting the temptation to look at Doug's page for about an hour, but ultimately gave in. She went to torment herself with his new profile photo again, but somehow it was back to the shot of the two of them. She blinked hard and wrinkled up her nose. What the hell was Doug doing now?

She put Tara's name into the search and couldn't find her, so she went to the old karate photo the school had posted, and Tara's name was no longer highlighted. She went to her messenger box and looked up Tara and while she could see their very old conversation from over a year ago about advice on a caterer for her daughter's high school graduation, she couldn't click on Tara or see her profile any more. Tara had blocked her, and for some reason that pissed Peach off almost more than anything else she had done, that fucking bitch.

A trilling buzz from the phone—Marny was texting her.

Marny: Well you had a hell of a night!

Huh? thought Peach.

Peach: How do u kno?

Marny: It's all over socials

Peach: What is?

Marny: Your romantic scene from the after
party! Look!

Then Marny sent screenshots from various social media platforms showing photos and snippets of videos labeled things like "romantic rescue at romance book convention" and "curvy midlife queen rescued by romance cover model."

Peach: Holy

Fucking

Shit

Holy shit!!!!!

Marny: I have an early client, call me later
tomorrow so we can talk!

Peach: yeah

Marny: Peachy?

Peach: yeah?

Marny: this is fucking awesome – git it gurl

Peach: I have no words

Marny: night!

Peach: night

Peach poked around the internet and found dozens of mentions of the incident and she was extremely thankful that she didn't have lots of social media for them to tag and find her. And that none of them seemed to have used her actual name. At least that.

She slammed the computer shut, found the remaining

rose creams and dug a couple of whiskies out of the mini bar. She crammed the chocolates in her mouth and washed them down with the little bottles and laid back and cried. She was glad she'd washed off all of her makeup because she would have gotten mascara all over the nice white comforter cover.

She saw the scene with Doug and Tara in her head over and over. She started to cry harder when her phone rang. It was almost eleven—Jesus, she hoped the kids were okay. She looked at her phone and it said "Do the Dougy" was calling. She sat upright, a lump in her throat, hot tears still stinging her eyes. She didn't want her marriage to be over, she just wanted it to be … better. Much better. She just couldn't be the only one who wanted to do the work. That would never fix anything, she was sure. She sent the call to voicemail.

She stared at the phone like it might do something. In about a minute the telltale bloop of a voicemail coming in sounded. She immediately picked it up and listened.

"Hi Peach. I am so sorry. I should have tried harder. Please let's talk. We can work this out."

She listened to it three times, her heart thudding harder each time. A montage of smiling Christmas moments, of anniversary celebrations, vacations, of cuddling on the couch with nachos watching zombie movies all flooded her mind. She loved Doug. She had loved him over half her life. But was that enough? She didn't know how long, if ever, she could get over the sense of betrayal. If she could ever trust him again.

One thing was certain: she'd have to get rid of her 600-thread-count Egyptian cotton anniversary sheets.

She tried to relax and go to sleep. She wanted to attend

the workshops and panels tomorrow with a clear mind. It would be her last day as an author and she planned to enjoy it and keep it in her heart forever. But every time she tried to close her eyes, her phone sounded with another text message from Doug, like "I'm sorry" and "sad face emoji" and "I would be willing to try therapy." That was the one that gave her some spark of hope. Even though it was after midnight and she wanted to be up at 7 a.m., she responded.

> Peach: You never wanted to do therapy before

> Dougy: Thank you for responding. I would like to now. I'm sorry. Just find a therapist and tell me when, and I'll come.

Peach paused for a moment. All of the hopeful feelings of repairing trust and finding new ground for their relationship evaporated. Doug didn't sound like he was about to take on any of this for himself, and for some reason that pissed her all the way off. She couldn't quite put her finger on it, but she knew her anger was righteous.

Or was it? He was offering to do therapy. Way too late, but he's willing. She put her phone on silent and picked up her laptop and opened up a fresh document and typed out "Desire Therapy" and started her second novel. She typed for three hours straight until she had to stop due to her neck and back aching, and remembered she had to be up in just a few short hours. She clicked the laptop closed and rolled over, and sleep quickly found her, dark and deep.

TEN

I'm No Author

Despite her long working night and short sleep, Peach woke up energized. She only gave a quick glance to the mirror before pulling on her curve-hugging jeans and the "Tea, Books & Me" tee she'd picked up a few years ago at a book fest. Today's workshops promised a nice casual energy that she found much more appealing than the suits and evening gowns and social smiles of the last two nights. Not that she minded smiling, exactly—it was second nature for Peach—but it was exhausting having to wear a face all the time, especially when you weren't feeling it.

She stuffed her laptop, pen and notebook into her tote and a minute later she was downstairs waiting to check in at Cassie Lair's workshop, wondering if there would be some snacks somewhere to get her through the morning. There seemed to be quite a buzz in the room, and she wondered if everybody was as charged up as she was. But as she looked around she saw a lot of people looking back, with smiles and waves and whispers to each other, and she realized it was probably because of last night.

Since Ryan had left her at her door, she had been hoping against hope that nobody would remember that little fiasco with the centerpiece flambé and the fire extinguisher, but it was clear now none of them would forget it. Ever. Her dreaded klutziness had become legend, immortalized in the annals of romance writer lore as The Night Romanticon Nearly Burned to the Ground. People would be telling their grandchildren about this, and she was pretty sure it was going to show up in a whole crop of novels—and, to be honest, she wasn't entirely sure that she hated the idea.

Regardless, she was determined to enjoy her last day as an author. In fact that was her mantra, should anything else go wrong: "I'm enjoying my last day as an author." Head up, shoulders back, badge in hand, she walked over to the coffee counter and found Laura nearby, smiling and chatting breezily with three other authors. Today she looked almost like a high school student in her jeans, white sneaks, and a black tee with a graphic of a typewriter and flowers and hearts coming out of it. Laura was wearing her hair loose and Peach admired the ginger cascade that fell over her shoulders and down to the middle of her back.

Peach grabbed a steaming cup of coffee, dumped in three creams and four packets of turbinado sugar, stirred it vigorously without incident, and took the six paces to Laura's group. She waved as she approached and Laura stopped mid-story, a huge smile spreading so wide that it seemed even her ears were participating. The others all paused to look at Peach, then started whispering to each other.

"Well, that was quite a demonstration you put on last night Peach!" Laura laughed. "How did they talk you into it?"

"I … wait, what? Who?" Peach tilted her head in confusion. She'd figured they were all waiting for some hot goss on Ryan Slate, but this was something else.

"You know, the models! They drafted you into one of their little romance enactments they do. It was so cute!" Laura enthused. "And what an honor for your first Romanticon! They don't do it every year."

"We loved it. Everybody ate it up!" said one of the other authors, a petite thirty-something blonde with a big smile and dimples, wearing various shades of pink right down to her cowgirl boots. "And with Ryan Slate too. Legend!" She fluttered her impossibly long eyelashes and took a sip from a blinged-out tumbler that read "Hot for Cowboys."

Finally it dawned on Peach what Ryan had actually done last night to save her—not just from being engulfed in flames, but from an enduring embarrassment that would have surely gone viral and dogged her for the rest of her life. *Okay, maybe that is being a tad overly dramatic,* she admitted to herself, *but Ryan really came through.* Peach smiled to herself, then nodded and tried to look oh-so-cool.

"Oh, yeah. They just asked me and I said why not, and that was that."

"What I wouldn't give!" said a middle-aged woman with a salt-and-pepper mop of hair, dressed in baggy jeans and a giant T-shirt printed with a tower of books and the slogan "Totally Stacked." Her voice sounded like a pack of cigarettes. "It looked so real, too. You're a pretty good actress, hon."

Peach smiled again and let out a nervous little laugh. "Yeah. Thanks."

The whole semicircle nodded in rapt unison, and Laura, a head taller than everybody else, gave Peach a thumbs up. At that moment Eryn came through the hall, checking her clipboard. She announced to everyone that the first panels would be starting in five minutes, and the little group disbanded with smiles and laughter. Laura sidled over to a somewhat dazed Peach.

"I'm heading down to the panel discussion on Generative AI and Copyright Infringement. Want to come?"

"Sounds … futuristic," smirked Peach. "Actually I'm taking your advice and I'm heading down to Cassie Lair's workshop on confidence and imposter syndrome."

"Oh hell yes, perfect! Well maybe I'll catch you at lunch then," Laura said with a wave, and headed off towards the ballroom—now partitioned into multiple spaces—while Peach went looking for Conference Room 101A.

Cassie Lair was not what Peach expected. She wasn't sure what she expected, maybe a thirty-something woman with an academic yet feminine aesthetic. Instead she found a woman who was possibly in her seventies, short, thin, with a fuzzy pink buzz cut. She sported plenty of black eyeliner, tight shiny black pants, black ankle boots with lots of buckles and a sleeveless Siouxsie and the Banshees tee. There was a tattoo of a pen with a squiggle line on her forearm and her fingers were loaded with gems and silver, as were her ears, which had at least six piercings each. Peach slid quietly into a chair at the very back corner of the room so as not to call attention to herself.

Cassie started out explaining that very few people actually finish a manuscript, and of those people, even fewer end up publishing. Not just because of gatekeeping at the big publishing houses, now that indie publishing had helped level the playing field, but because, as she put it, "It's a lot of fucking work. People think writing sounds like play time. Well it is not. Is it gratifying? Yes. But that doesn't mean it's not work." From there she delved into finding the strength to shut down the negative voices in your head.

As much as the workshop wisdom itself, Peach enjoyed the classroom atmosphere—the other people typing away, the sound of pens scratching on paper, the feel of her own pen indenting the pages of her notebook with her looping scrawl. There was something scholastic about it, something essential, and she hadn't realized how much she had missed it, and had in fact been longing for it. She wrote in the margin, "the magic of a fresh box of school supplies in September."

The class was only an hour and a quarter, not really long enough for anything but a bit of a shove to get you headed in the right line of thinking about yourself and your work. At one point Cassie asked for everybody in the room who was an author to raise their hands, and all but three of them did. Peach figured she wasn't very visible back there, sunk down in her seat, so it didn't much matter if she raised her hand or not. Likely no one would even notice. But Cassie Lair clearly did notice, because at the end of the session she said, "Dawson, Sondra, and Peach, please come see me before you head out."

Peach felt like the high school principal had just said her name over the P.A. Her heart did a couple of thuds and her face flushed, but she scooped up her bag and her notebook and waited at the front of the room. Cassie Lair rounded the lecture table to face the trio directly, arms crossed, sizing them up.

"The three of you are here, presumably, to work on your writing craft. Yes?"

Peach bit her lip, Dawson shifted from one foot to the other, Sondra fidgeted her pen. It was like watching a group of teenagers caught smoking in school. Peach figured Cassie enjoyed playing teacher and thought of them as low hanging fruit.

"Good. Now, I suggest you shit or get off the pot, and I mean that in the nicest way possible." Peach thought she saw her expression shift ever so subtly from judge to counselor. "You can go to a hundred of these things. Spend thousands of dollars, finish a dozen manuscripts. You might even get published. But until you can see yourself as an author you will take no joy in it. Eventually you will be crying over your keyboard with a bottle of whiskey, wishing you had the courage to stand up and say who you really are. So do it. Do it now. Commit to the idea. Or just take up crochet or something. You're dismissed."

With that Cassie snapped up her black tote—complete with a Jolly Roger flag stitched on it—and exited, stage left. The three penitents were left standing there, awkwardly absorbing the scolding and the lesson. They made brief, guilty eye contact with each other before shuffling out of the room.

Peach headed straight to the lunch area, where a dozen tables had been set out and a buffet was laid with sandwiches, snacks, fruit and veggie trays, and drinks. She got in line with all the other, more carefree attendees, collected her turkey sandwich, ripple chips, cookie, and tea, and went to an empty table to munch and sulk.

She pulled out her notebook and flipped through it while pecking at her food, not much in the mood to eat. But it would be a long day and she didn't want her blood sugar to bottom out. She kept getting sidetracked by thoughts of Ryan, which made her feel all fluttery in her stomach, but she was determined to focus her efforts on her writing notes. She looked for a new page to write down some feelings and saw her note from yesterday: "This is a dumb list because you aren't an author and this will never be your life." Reading it now stung in a way she didn't expect.

Maybe it was just all that had happened in the past week. Maybe it was that this world of authors and personalities seemed so removed from the one she knew, and even though she wanted a life of champagne and roses, she would only ever be a chardonnay and tiger lilies kind of girl.

She nibbled at her sandwich and kept looking at the self-defeating, dream-deflating note. She didn't even notice at first that Laura had sat down with her own lunch a couple of seats over. It seemed to her that Laura was picking up on her mood.

"You okay?" Laura asked, then took a small bite of her sandwich and a sip of diet cola.

Peach shrugged.

"Ohhh, wait … Did you not raise your hand when Cassie asked if you were an author?" She took another bite of her sandwich, this time followed with a potato chip.

Peach finally looked at her more directly.

"Oh you know about that, huh?"

"Oh, yes ma'am," she said, still crunching. "You're looking at a past victim, year three of Rambling Romanticon."

Peach let out an ironic half-laugh. "Well, glad I'm not alone, at least." She pushed aside her notebook and got down to her lunch. It somehow made her feel better that this whole thing was some kind of tradition, almost like she'd endured an initiation of sorts.

"You're definitely not alone, Peach. Don't be shy in her classes, it never ends well. You might feel like you can hide out in the back, but I almost think she pays more attention to those people." Laura popped one last bite of sandwich in her mouth, dusted her hands and put her eyebrows up, prompting Peach for some response.

"Noted," Peach said, and sipped her tea thoughtfully. "How long is this break anyway?"

"An hour. Plenty of time to contemplate your entire future." Laura smiled broadly, but Peach's smile was small and uncertain, much like her spirit at this moment.

More people had filtered in and the tables were filling up; there was now a low hum of gentle lunch conversation. Some people ate quietly and wrote notes, while others sat in groups discussing whatever workshop they had just taken. Laura pulled out a notebook.

"I'm going to just sit here to take some notes myself, if you don't mind the company."

"I'm glad for it," Peach assured her. "And I appreciate you, Laura—this whole weekend. Really, thanks for making the new girl feel welcome."

"Aww, thanks babe. Glad to do it. I must say, this Romanticon has been un-for-gettable." She grinned cheerfully, flipped open her notebook and clicked a pen, but never got to using it. Some sort of commotion was brewing at the entrance to the lunch area.

A young woman Peach recognized as the volunteer who was flirting with Ryan was backing into the room and holding up her hands in a futile gesture of restraint.

"Sir! Sir, I'm sorry, but if you aren't registered you cannot come in here." She finally grabbed the walkie on her hip and said, "Eryn, we need assistance in the lunch area with an unauthorized entry. We may need security."

"Roger that," Eryn's voice squawked over the walkie. "I'm on my way."

One of the male authors had lined up with the young volunteer and was saying something like, "Hey man, you heard the lady," when a raised voice cut through the chatter and made Peach's eyes bug out.

"I just need to talk to my wife for just a minute. It's important. I won't be long, I swear."

Peach stood and craned her neck to see Doug pushing his way through the thickening crowd. He was looking around wildly, clutching a bunch of tiger lilies wrapped with a giant yellow bow. He soon locked eyes on her and they stared at each other for a moment, then he walked quickly in her direction with the young volunteer and several others in his wake. Doug sidestepped one last confrontational author and held out the flowers toward Peach, who stared at them but didn't take them. His would-be pursuers also stopped, unsure what to do next but apparently deciding he was harmless.

"I know you probably thought I forgot tiger lilies were your favorite." He thrust the bouquet a bit further towards her but she still didn't take it, just blinked at him. He was wearing the suit that their daughters had given him for Father's Day several years ago, and the tie she'd given him for his last birthday—silk, in the perfect shade of blue that brought out his eyes. He laid the flowers on the table.

"Peach, you look amazing." He took her in from head to toe. "It's not just your hair either, something else is different."

More people were filling the room, and Peach saw Laura standing close by, facing Doug in a stance that said she was ready to stick one of those impossibly long arms out and bop him one in the chops if she had to. Peach loved her for this, but she also knew it wasn't necessary. Doug was not a violent man, just a rather thick one.

He'd flown out to Maryland to bring her flowers! Between his affair with Tara and now this bullheaded attempt to reconcile, he was the most animated and vital Peach had seen him in a long, long time.

"Please, Peach—Baby? Can't we just talk?"

Laura caught her eye and whispered, "What a weekend, hey?"

Peach suppressed a laugh that would have been totally inappropriate at that moment, and tried to contemplate her future. She realized this was one of those before-and-after moments, and she unexpectedly thought of the Helping Hands in the movie *Labyrinth*, making young Sarah choose whether she wanted to go "Up, or Down?"

She could feel the crowd holding their collective breath. She was pretty sure if she rebuffed Doug right now, after he made such a big effort and in front of all these people, their marriage would never recover. Not a snowball's chance. So was she really ready to completely give up on thirty-plus years together?

That was when Eryn strode into the hall—all in black, walkie in hand—flanked by two rather large and unsmiling gentlemen. She did not look happy. The crowd parted as the three approached Doug. Eryn pointed toward the entrance with her walkie.

"Sir, I want you out of my convention. Now."

Doug looked deflated. His eyes swept the room like he knew he didn't belong there. He gave Peach one last look and turned back toward the glass doors. Peach didn't know if she should let him leave the convention feeling as hurt and lonely as she did just a few days ago, or follow him out and maybe take one step toward saving their marriage. Their problems couldn't be all his fault, could they? Didn't she owe it to their family and all their years together to at least see if there was any chance at all?

She scooped up her things—though not the tiger lilies— and followed the security men as they escorted Doug to the door. And she realized that, once again, she was walking through a crowd of gawking and whispering authors. Were they fascinated? Were they judging her? She couldn't tell, but she couldn't really think about that right now. One thing was for sure, they probably wouldn't forget her anytime soon.

Once they were outside of the hotel, standing in the bright afternoon sun, she looked at her husband and saw how haggard he appeared. Not just because he was nearly sixty, mind you, but because he probably hadn't eaten or slept since she last saw him. They needed to get out of the sun, so she headed toward an overhang that promised a bit of shade, and Doug followed her like a puppy. She turned around to face him and crossed her arms. He wore a sheepish expression, as if he were a boy who'd lost his best friend. Peach wondered if that would be her or Tara— because she was pretty sure based on Facebook context clues that Tara had kicked him to the curb. Or at least gave him some kind of ultimatum.

"I have another class soon," Peach said coolly, giving no hint of her aching heart and the sappy sentimental memories of her husband and family that were flooding her mind. Doug proposing at Waterside in Norfolk, Virginia. Doug bringing her breakfast in bed for a dozen Mother's Days, and making love in a tent in the Adirondacks. Doug rubbing cocoa butter on her belly when she was pregnant, and talking to their baby through her bellybutton. A thousand sweet moments. She was stern on the outside, acting like a tough cookie, but she was starting to feel a little gooey on the inside.

He looked down at his shoes and rubbed the back of his neck, then looked back at her.

"I know I completely screwed up. I know that. I wanted

to tell you in person how sorry I am, and what a cock-up this all was."

Peach balled up her face like she smelled something rancid, and he winced.

"Sorry, bad choice of words."

"Yeah, no kidding," Peach replied.

He stepped a little closer to her and put his hands out in a pleading manner, and Peach recognized it as the same hangdog expression he made when she would forget to buy his ice cream sandwiches.

"Peach, I love you. I know I lost sight of that, and I'm so, so sorry. If you could find it in your heart to forgive me, I promise I'll do better. I'll take you out every month for a nice dinner, and I'll do the dishes without being asked. I'll even plan, like, birthday parties and stuff you've been wanting help with. Anything to make it up to you."

And then Peach remembered that for all those bright and beautiful moments, there were so many more where she was quietly ignored, burdened with the household duties, solely responsible for the kids, and felt totally overlooked and forgotten. Why would it take somebody thirty years to start being supportive? Why would you wait until things were totally broken before you decided to do something? She suspected that Melissa would say "it's the patriarchy," and she figured that Doug's "man training" was certainly one aspect. But he was a grown man, and he knew when he wasn't treating her like she was important. Her needs didn't matter, until now. Until he was losing her.

She also wasn't buying the pleading sincerity. She'd seen it before—when he promised to take the trash out without being asked, and would do it for three weeks and then not do it for months. Then she would get frustrated and remind him and he would say she was needling him all the time. Or when he discovered online porn and would leave her lying in bed lonely while he jerked off to some stranger on the internet. After Peach had a major meltdown, he promised to at least cut back, and come to bed, and try harder to be close. That would go in cycles too. It had been years of Peach feeling second best, shut out, sometimes totally alone in a house full of people. She guessed she was probably still second best even now, and that he'd only come crawling back because Tara had cut him loose.

"What happened with Tara, Doug?" She unfolded her arms.

"Do we have to talk about her?" he asked.

Peach rolled her eyes so hard her whole head went with them.

"Oh? Am I making you uncomfortable, Doug? Yes! We absolutely have to talk about Tara!" Peach heard herself yelling and reflexively started looking around to see if anybody was in earshot. But then she thought, *Fuck it, let 'em hear this.* She wasn't surprised to see there were a few faces pressed to the window glass, watching them.

Doug's shoulders slumped and he let out a big sigh. He put his hands on his head and turned to sit on the bench behind them. Finally he gave up a big dramatic shrug.

"She dumped me, okay? Okay? Are you happy? She dumped me."

"So is that why you're here?" Peach's tone flattened, and the embers in her chest started to fizzle out.

Doug looked up wearing a wounded expression.

"No, of course not, Peach! You think that little of me?"

Again with that pleading tone and his "where are my ice cream sandwiches?" face. Those glowing memories were turning to cold ash.

"So you're saying if Tara hadn't dumped you, you'd honestly still be here right now? Begging to be with me?" She watched Doug's forehead wrinkle as he contemplated the best way to answer. *Spoiler alert, Dougy boy: there is no good way to answer.*

"Okay, well if I'm being honest I might not be here today, but I would be eventually. Tara and I weren't right for each other. I just went crazy or something. I don't know how to explain it. You don't like anything I like. You nag me all the time about such small stuff. Maybe we can talk about that in counseling. If you didn't nag me, I wouldn't feel so beat down, then I would feel more like being intimate. Y' know?" He looked like a man who had just experienced a moment of clarity and was imparting some vital marriage-saving wisdom.

She wanted to laugh in his stupid hopeful face, but just bowed and shook her head, incredulous.

"Doug, you realize …" she began, but looked at him and finally saw that it wouldn't matter what she said, he would never hear her. He could never grasp the irony of him calling her a nag instead of deeming himself lazy and uncaring, never see why her having to check up on him meant she was still doing the work. *Huh. What a sweet gig that is for men, to both not do the thing, but also get to be mad that you ask them to do the thing, and say you're the problem.* Rather than try to explain concepts like unseen labor and patriarchal privilege and all of that to poor befuddled Doug, she instead addressed his complaint that she didn't like anything he likes.

"Nachos. Zombie movies. Bicycling. Waterfalls. Kenny Rogers. German chocolate cake. Ferris wheels. Coffee shops in small towns. Beaches in the off-season. *Star Wars*—but only the originals because Han shot first. Scrabble. Lazy

Sunday mornings. Pancake breakfasts and spaghetti dinners at the fire hall. Shall I go on?"

Doug's face clouded over and his energy shifted from desperation to what appeared to be true remorse, and something deeper was swimming in his eyes now.

"Peach, I'm so sorry. You didn't deserve what I did to you."

She gave a small knowing nod, her brow holding the weight of what was left of her feelings for him.

"You're right, I didn't."

"I swear, if you give me another chance I will make up for all the things I didn't do. All the things I ignored."

"I think it's too little, too late, Doug." She heard Johnny Mathis and Deniece Williams singing the words in her head. Doug looked like he wanted to protest, but she was right and he knew it, and arguing against the point would only confirm what she said. He put his hands up in surrender.

"You didn't do anything wrong. You have been a great wife. I'm the one who messed up, and I'm sorry." He heaved an enormous sigh. "I'll leave you to your convention. And Peach …"

She waited quietly for another cycle of begging to ramp up.

"I know I'm a selfish bastard, and it will be hard to believe me when I say this, but I am rooting for you. I wish you the very best."

"Thank you, Doug."

He nodded back and walked away into the parking lot and she watched him go. She had felt more seen by him in these last few moments than she had in years, but there was no tug in her heart to follow him. Then Peach hightailed it to Cassie Lair's plotting workshop, where she knew she absolutely would raise her hand this time.

ELEVEN

A Band of Gold

Feeling like she might one day learn how to get out of her own way after having a second Cassie Lair workshop under her belt, Peach joined Laura for a session about building your author brand through online presence. They followed that with a panel discussion on the different levels of heat in romance, so they were more than ready for the long break with heavy appetizers and a cash bar, which would then lead into the closing mixer of the evening. Attendees were encouraged to grab a cocktail and trade business cards, bid on silent auction items, and drop raffle tickets into glass bowls in hopes of winning various prizes.

Peach stood behind Laura in line for drinks, and watched the bartender at work. He had a tattoo that ran up his neck and into his hair, which was mostly black with shots of gray running through it. But what intrigued her was how practiced he was, with little flourishes of graceful movement as he grabbed and poured from the bottles and taps surrounding him.

"Tequila sunrise, please," Laura said to the bartender.

"Old school, I like it," he acknowledged, and shot her a grin he'd surely shot many a woman over a bar.

"Oh, that sounds good, I'll have one too," Peach said and smiled at Laura. "Haven't had one of those in years! I was actually too young when they were really popular, but my parents sure liked them. I would've expected somebody your age to ask for a Negroni Sbagliato or something." She laughed at her own mangled pronunciation. "Isn't that what the kids are drinking these days?"

Laura threw her head back and laughed, merrily thanked the bartender and dropped a couple of bills in his jar. She slid Peach's drink to her and they headed off in search of a table.

"Girl, first of all, don't you know the Seventies are cool again? I got the recipe off of a website for a Seventies party I threw last year, and just happen to love them. And second of all, how old do you think you are?"

Peach considered the question for a moment. She just figured her age was obvious.

"I'm pretty old," she said flatly as they found a small table not far from a smattering of authors who were otherwise engaged in conversation.

"I think you think about your age more than anybody seeing you does." Laura plucked the maraschino cherry from her drink and sucked it off of the stem, chewing it slowly as she regarded Peach with a questioning eye.

"Well I feel old as dirt. Aging is weird. Your skin starts to change, then your hair goes gray. The people you see out in the world get younger and younger, and they treat you like you don't have anything to offer. After a while it makes you start to think they're right."

"I think you have plenty to offer," Laura replied, and

took another sip of her sunrise. "Oh my god this drink is so good. Drink!"

Peach tipped back her glass, crushed ice rattling. "Shit. That's yummy."

"Yeah. We might need more than one." Laura's tone got a little more serious. "So …"

Peach tilted her head and lowered one brow. "Yes?"

"Do you suppose I'll see you around at some other romance conventions?"

Peach looked down at her drink and contemplated all that had happened in the past five days and the year before that. She looked around the room at the authors all drinking and chatting, smiling and relaxed. Everybody had been kind of buttoned up and businessy for the convention—with some notable exceptions on the first night dance floor—but now in the home stretch they were letting their hair down a little, and a more relaxed vibe pulsed through the room.

She really did something big this weekend, and got a glimpse of another life, a life she might have had. She remembered feeling this sense of accomplishment when she had finished a school project, or pulled off an event that made her kids really happy. But something still didn't fit her quite right. She'd made friends with Laura—or rather Laura made friends with her—but there were so many other conversations going on that she couldn't make heads or tails of.

"I still don't feel like I know what I'm doing," she sighed.

"That will pass, I promise you, with time and more books published." Laura tried waving to the bartender for another round. "Listen, I'm going to Sandy Cheeks at the Beach Romanticon in September, down in Virginia Beach. They're still taking registrations. I checked." She wrinkled up her chin and raised her brows. "How 'bout it, Peachy?"

Peach blinked a few times, a whirlwind of ideas and possibilities flooding her mind. A big table display, new swag, new clothes, smiling authors, beach waves. Seafood! It was so tempting—so what was it she was afraid of?

Before Peach could reply she felt an insistent tap on her shoulder. She turned around and saw Rose Ramble standing there, looking at her with an expectant expression. Peach was stunned, but determined to keep her wits about her. She wasn't sure what Rose Ramble could be expecting from her exactly, but imagined it was along the lines of *Hello* and *I'm so sorry your convention made a mistake and allowed me to register, but I'm glad I'm here.*

"Ms. Ramble! So nice to meet you! I'm—"

"Peach Kincaid. Yes, I think everybody here knows your name by now." Rose smiled, showing a little bit of teeth. She seemed to be gently teasing, and that was how Peach was choosing to take it, because inside she was in a complete panic. She opted for a sincere but not too desperate apology.

"I'm so sorry I've disrupted your event with all of my personal drama …"

"My dear," Rose said grandly, "I think we call that romance." She let a big smile spread across her face and reached out to shake her hand, and Peach took it, feeling very proud of herself, though she was not entirely sure why.

"I suppose we do," Peach laughed. "I am really sorry I didn't contact your administrative staff about the mistake."

Rose gave a small shake of her head, her black hair and red rose adornment swaying a little. "And what mistake would that be?" she asked as they released hands.

Peach gestured wide to encompass everything around them. "My name on the list? My being here? I probably took some poor deserving author's place. And it won't happen again, because I'm not really cut out to be an author. But I'm sorry I didn't say something, even if I absolutely loved the entire weekend. So thank you for that."

"Oh, Peach. I loved your book *Greyson Edging*. I was glad to see the team was able to get you registered. No mistake my dear. Very deserved. Fantastic debut. Keep going."

Peach couldn't have been more astounded if she had woken up at the bottom of the ocean as a mermaid in Neptune's castle.

"I … Well, I don't know what to say. I think that …" She was blabbering, and Laura lightly elbowed her. "Thank you. Thank you so much for the opportunity!"

"We pride ourselves in taking on at least one promising new romance author per year and being their debut event. And from what we've seen this weekend, I'd say you have a lot of promise, Peach. So glad you could be with us."

Peach's entire year was made in that one moment—all the basement writing, the finding an editor, the printing, the fights with Doug—it was all worth it. She was walking on a cloud.

"Please send me an ARC when you finish the next one," Rose said.

"I will … I'll do that, thank you. Thank you!" Peach replied.

"Wonderful. Well, you ladies enjoy yourself. I've got to circulate, you know." Rose Ramble strode away coolly around the bar atop her tall, impossibly thin stilettos.

"Oh my *god*!" Peach exclaimed in the loudest whisper she could. Laura tipped back her glass and finished off her drink

"So, madame author? I believe you were about to say something like, "Yes, Laura, I'll definitely see you at Sandy Cheeks'.""

Peach laughed. "Well it would be downright rude if I

didn't pursue my writing career after that, right? I mean, it would be like spitting in the face of a demigoddess or something."

"I would say yes. I'm going to have to read that book of yours, PK."

"I am an author," Peach said with a dreamy look on her face.

"Damn straight you are! Now, let's score two more tequila sunrises!"

Rose Ramble had read her book and liked it—really liked it. Cassie Lair might have insisted that Peach look inward for validation, but right or wrong, that one affirming voice made all the difference in helping her see herself as a real author, and she felt almost dizzy with possibilities. She knew she was still in over her head, but she no longer felt like she was drowning—more like taking a plunge.

The night was young so they nursed those second drinks a lot longer. Peach indulged in tiny heart-shaped cookies and pondered her unexpected future in writing while Laura offered advice on her next steps. And there was something else Peach was feeling bolder about. She was looking hopefully around the room to see if the models were a part of the evening event, and when she didn't spot them she thought to ask one of the volunteers. When she couldn't find any of them either, she realized they might not be on the agenda for the closing mixer since it was more casual and the convention was winding down. Laura swirled the last drops of her drink in her glass.

"I'm going to swing by the bar again and then go talk to my friend Casey and her crew over there. Want to join me?"

"Thanks, I think I'll stick around here and have another heart cookie."

"Were you maybe hoping to see Ryan here?" Laura

chuckled conspiratorially. "I thought I saw you craning your neck. But no, the models don't do the closing, they've all been off duty since last night."

Peach felt more sad than she'd expected to when she realized she probably wouldn't see Ryan again. She gave Laura a noncommittal shrug.

"However …" Laura continued. She was looking over Peach's left shoulder and quietly pointed a finger. It was Ryan, dressed in what were likely his regular clothes, similar to the ones she first met him in. When Peach made eye contact, he smiled. She immediately smiled back, maybe a little bigger and goofier than she meant to. He sauntered over to the table.

"Well, hi there," he greeted her in that warm baritone.

"Hi," Peach returned, gazing at him and still smiling. Maybe it was the cocktails, but it seemed like the room got soft around the edges, and the hum of people talking became muffled and distant. Laura said something to Ryan and laughed from miles away. She got up to go see her friends while Peach sat there and smiled with her whole body. Ryan took a seat.

"I hoped you'd still be here, Peach. I booked an extra night just in case."

"You booked an extra night, just in case … I was still here?" She was still smiling but confused.

"I did." He said it so matter-of-factly.

"For me?"

"Yes, for you. Is that so hard to believe?"

She puffed up her cheeks and blew out, blushing a little.

"Honestly, yeah, it kind of is."

"Well, that's awful. That you doubt yourself like that."

"Maybe so. But if I told you all the reasons why, you'd

go running in the other direction. Pretty sure it would make me sound massively insecure. And uninteresting."

Ryan gently placed his hand over hers.

"Or, and hear me out, maybe it wouldn't?"

Peach could almost see him searching for a way through her blockade, and she loved how hard he was trying to reach her.

"How about this, Peach—let's just sit here and talk. Just talk. In fact I made a list of the things I most wanted to know about you. I mean, there are way more things I want to know about you, but I thought a small starter list might make it more fun and less scary."

She broke eye contact and her smile faded. "Oh, you think I'm scared?" she said in an oddly mocking tone.

He softened. "Aren't you? You're at least nervous. Though I can't imagine why."

Peach narrowed her eyes. "Okay, maybe. But I think you can imagine why if you try and put yourself in my shoes."

"How about if I just show you the list? Would you mind? We can take it from there."

His face was so warm, so gorgeous and sincere in the daylight—and so close, she could see the slight crinkling around his eyes. But this new, more confident Peach was also a wary one.

"Ryan, I don't think I'm ready to get my feelings all tangled up about somebody. Not even somebody as hot as you." She sure wanted to, though.

He nodded. Then there was that dreadful dead air. She had never had to fill dead air with Doug, or most other men for that matter, as they were often talking about themselves. But Ryan didn't seem defeated, or even disappointed. He was just looking at her. Into her. His face calm and waiting, as if he had all the time in the world for her.

Peach, however, couldn't stand the quiet gathering between them for one more second.

"Okay, let me see the list. But I am only going to answer the stuff I want to answer."

He leaned back and grinned. "I wouldn't want it any other way," he said. His blue, gray and white plaid shirt looked so soft she wanted to lay her head against it. He pulled a slip of paper out of his breast pocket, unfolded it and handed it to her.

She held his eyes with hers just a moment longer, then looked down at the paper, having no idea what to expect.

Things I would like to know about Peach Kincaid:
Favorite color or colors (just one can be so limiting)
Favorite flower
The perfect date night
The perfect birthday celebration
Favorite comfort food
Favorite band (or top three, if it's too hard to choose)
First concert and favorite concert
If you won the lottery, what is the first thing you'd buy just for yourself?

He leaned back and rested his hands in his lap, relaxing into the moment.

"So, not too scary, right? It's not super long, just a place to start."

Peach gave a quiet sniff then looked up at him and blinked away a tear.

"Oh, no …!" Ryan looked genuinely concerned. He sat

up straight and pulled a folded blue bandana out of his other shirt pocket and dabbed at her cheek. "Why are there tears? There aren't supposed to be tears."

"I don't … I'm not sure." She took the bandana when he held it out to her and she wiped away her tears and half her makeup onto it. She looked up at him apologetically.

"Sorry."

The bandana left the smell of him on her face, and she felt like a teenager with a moony crush. Ryan let out a small chuckle and leaned in to share her space. He put his big warm hand on her soft chilly one.

"It's okay, Peach," he said with a sympathetic smile, and waited quietly for her to work out why she was feeling sad. She sniffed.

"I think it's because nobody has asked me things like this in so long."

He nodded and stayed close. Peach could feel an enveloping safe energy emanating from him, but she didn't trust it. She couldn't help thinking this was all some kind of prank or a ploy. He might have seen something in her when they first met. A vulnerability? An easy target? Was her low self-esteem broadcasting that much?

"This doesn't seem real," she admitted.

"Mm. I think that's your hungry tired soul talking. I think you imagine somebody who looks like me—which, granted I am kind of hot …" he gave her a teasing wink and a chuckle, "… that I would only look at other models. But trust me, all of the stuff that comes with this job, the emphasis on appearances, it can make you long for something more real. Besides, you're gorgeous, Peach. I'm sure you've gotten plenty of attention in your life. You're just … you're a little out of practice. You'll find yourself again, if you're looking."

Peach shrugged. "It just feels like a setup somehow. Like there are hidden cameras. This model at Romanticon giving me all kinds of flirty helpfulness. I just remember somewhere in the back of my high school brain, Denny Jenkins saying he liked to go after fat girls and shy girls because their self esteem was shot and they were more likely to let you in their pants." That sounded way worse out loud than she imagined it would.

"First of all, gross. What a horrible little gremlin Denny Jenkins must have been. Hope he grew out of that. And second, high school was a long time ago. For both of us, Peach. I'm more than a pretty face …" he fluttered his eyelashes with a smirk, "… and you're more than a middle-aged mom with a cheatin' husband. Way more."

For a man so invested in his looks, Ryan certainly had a lot going on under the surface, and Peach recognized that, from the beginning, he had treated her like a whole person. Maybe he really did see something in her. Why was that so hard to believe? It's not like she felt she was ugly exactly, just … not her best. And it wasn't the cellulite or the gray hair, it was because her whole sense of self-worth had been handed over for decades, subsumed by motherhood and service to her husband—not to mention the lack of passion for so many years—until she began to see herself as nothing special. So she learned to get comfy in sweats, and let her hair go natural, which was cheaper anyway, and live without passion.

And that, she realized, was the danger of opening up to Ryan Slate. What if he made her believe she could have passion in her life again, only to find it was all a gag? This wasn't like a romance novel she could indulge in and then put safely back on her shelf. For Peach, the stakes were sky high. If Ryan wasn't for real, it would be devastating.

But he was here, and he was looking at her, really looking, and he was seeing so much she had forgotten about herself. How could she walk away without at least giving it a chance? Which would be the greater regret—finding it wasn't real, or never knowing?

She coolly ran her finger through the condensation on the side of her glass, then traced the rim of it slowly, thoughtfully.

"So, you didn't think I was all vulnerable and easy pickings? You don't go from con to con wooing middle-aged women with low self-esteem like a high school gremlin with no conscience?"

He scooted his chair over and leaned in, inches from her. His low voice, so close to her ear, made her whole body vibrate.

"I'm sorry I didn't get a chance to tell you this the other night. You were clearly nervous when we first met. Your purse had thrown all of your personal stuff onto the floor in front of so many other authors—people who were your peers, whose perception of you was important. It would be embarrassing for anybody, and that's why I wanted to help. But then you didn't back off or go home, you kept your place in line and stepped up to the counter anyway and finished what you started. That combination of brave and cute, it was sexy. I was hooked right away." The right side of his mouth smiled, so crooked and kissable.

Her face softened, and she opened a little more to him.

"Cute and sexy, huh?" She liked to think of somebody seeing her that way. She was so used to being ignored, or told something was wrong with her. Men tended to treat her like an old lady now, even those older than her. Young women looked past her like she wasn't there, and after a while she really did feel invisible. She'd heard people say that getting older was like that, but she didn't realize it could start when she still felt so young inside, when there were still so many things she wanted to do and be—especially after her thirty-year hiatus from herself.

She leaned in closer, her hair brushing her chin, her cranberry-glossed lips aching to pull all the way in for a kiss, but not wanting to do that in such a public place. Especially after the scene she'd given everybody last night. Instead she touched the tip of her nose to his—sweetly, playfully—then leaned back again and smiled.

"Okay. I'll answer one of these per day. And if you still want to talk to me after I've answered all of them, I will buy a ticket to the next conference you'll be at. That will give us a little space to think about things and it'll give you time to decide if you can date a woman who likes … the Bee-Gees." She gave a few innocent blinks.

Ryan made a face that looked like he wouldn't dream of dating someone who listened to the Bee-Gees, but it quickly dissolved into a guilty grin.

"*Spirits Having Flown* was literally the first album I ever owned. I bought it with my tips from the pizza shop."

Her face lit up with delighted recognition. "Get out! You must have been like two years old when that album came out."

"I was one year old when my parents discovered that the *Saturday Night Fever* soundtrack made me jump around in my bouncer. After Mom gave me their old record player I thought I'd try another Bee-Gees album to see how I liked it, and I wore it out. I had to get a second copy."

"Okay, I can relate to that. Do you like E.L.O.?"

He put his hands flat on the table with mock gravitas. "I *love* E.L.O."

"I'll bet you're Mr. Blue Sky," she laughed. "So you're

into oldies, but how do you feel about … hmm … Rufus Wainwright?" She always remembered her daughter singing along with his music video. Ryan's eyebrows lifted.

"Wow, did not expect that one. 'Cigarettes and Chocolate Milk'? When I heard that song I bought the CD."

They were both smiling sweetly at this point, their energies flowing and warm. This felt so natural, so honest, she decided she could chance a step into pre-relationship territory.

"Can I ask you to do something for me?" This was going to be a test. A test of how much energy Ryan was willing to put into this thing, whatever it was, or might be. She wanted to see just how interested he actually was.

"I would love to do something for you."

"Would you make me a playlist of some of your favorite songs for me to listen to while I write?"

"I will absolutely make you a playlist of my favorite songs. I'll send it to you."

She gave him a bit of side eye. "We'll see." *Do not have any expectations, Peach,* she warned herself, but her heart was hopeful and her tummy butterflies were no help at all.

"I know I should probably bid you adieu and let you finish up your Romanticon weekend," Ryan said, and Peach's heart sank a bit. "But right now I'd really like to dance with you." He held out his big hand, waiting. She couldn't hide her confusion.

"But … there's no music tonight."

"Not down here there isn't. But I have a suite upstairs with bluetooth speakers and a minibar—if you'd like to dance with me?" His eyes were calling to her, and it made her thighs vibrate. But then Peach felt a slight sense of panic, a swirl of good and bad filling her up that made her forget about her vibrating thighs for a moment.

"I'm sorry, Ryan … could you excuse me for just a moment? I promise I'll be right back." She said it so politely, it sounded almost cold to her ears.

"Of course. I didn't mean to put any pressure on you, Peach. Take your time." He stood when she stood, and watched her walk to the alcove where the restrooms were. She saw him sit back down as she went around the corner.

Peach, now completely out of her depth at the thought of even a potential physical romance with this man, dialed the one person she could count on to straighten out her tangled mind. She paced in the women's restroom as the phone rang, more and more worried it would go to voicemail. "Pick up dammit!" she hissed into the phone. At last, Marny picked up.

"Hey Peach, what's shakin'? Did you have the best time ever? You better say yes, because I'm living a little vicariously …"

"Marny! Please listen to me carefully, I don't have a lot of time." She was still pacing the restroom lounge. "Okay, it's been a crazy weekend and I'm sorry I didn't keep you up to date like I promised. It's just been go-go-go the whole time. First, Rose Ramble read my book and she liked it! My goddam hero! I really wish you could have been here to give me an 'I told you so'."

"Woah, that's so …"

"That's how I ended up here—she wanted me! She made it happen! I can't even believe it. But then, you would not believe the scene that Doug caused."

"Doug?"

"Yes! He flew out here and brought me flowers and begged for me to forgive him."

"That smelly little goat turd! The nerve!"

"I know, right? But Marny? Marny … Ryan Slate wants

to take me up to his suite, play the Bee-Gees for me, and dance while we partake of his minibar."

Peach heard only silence.

"Marny? That's insane, right? I'm crazy if I do that. Right?"

"Jesus Peach, what the hell kind of witchcraft have you been up to?"

"I don't know. I must have used too much mugwort or something? This is a lot, girl—what do I do?"

Marny inhaled loudly.

"First, did you forgive Doug?"

"Oh, hell no. I told him to get bent. Well, in my own way."

"Okay. Next … Wait, I have to rinse this bleach out of my hair or it's gonna set my scalp on fire."

"Uggh! Dammit Marny, why you gotta be bleaching your hair right now!"

"Sorry, didn't know you were gonna have a hunk booty call emergency. Hang on!"

It felt like an eternity before Marny came back. Peach was so worked up she thought she might pee her pants. Good thing she was already in the bathroom.

"Okay, I'm back. Whew. Peach, look, if you're asking me what you should do, I can't say. I can only tell you what I would probably do, and if you're sure he's not a serial murderer, I would absolutely be grinding to Bee-Gees with a romance cover model if that situation ever happened to come up for me. Which it won't, but I'm betting you never thought it would come up for you either."

"I did not."

"Go back out there and say yes to the things that make you happy."

"Even if they are selfish?"

"Yes. I repeat, go back out there and say yes to the things that make you happy."

"You're right," Peach said, nodding even though Marny wasn't there to see it. "That's advice I probably wouldn't have listened to a week ago."

"I know. Girl, live your dreams. Love you. And text me later!"

"Love you too!"

Peach dropped the phone in her purse, ducked into a bathroom stall, and took out her little freshen-up wipes. They were lime coconut, and were supposed to not just make you smell nice, but taste nice too—not a feature she bought them for, but it sure felt like a bonus right now. Maybe. Probably. She pulled out her mini travel cologne and gave a spritz to her panties and underarms. Then touched up her lip gloss, crunched a mint, and headed back to the table where she found Ryan.

He was nursing what looked like a Manhattan and tapping the rim of the glass with a silver band he had on his right middle finger, waiting. There was something very old fashioned and irresistibly sexy about the whole scene. He smiled and stood as soon as he saw her. She gave a gentle grin and leaned in towards his ear.

"Let's go talk in your suite," she said with a soft sultry smile.

A glimmer of desire crept from Ryan's eyes to his mouth, then his tongue made a lovely subtle lick of his bottom lip. He threw back the rest of his Manhattan, set the glass on the table and put out his hand, which Peach took after only the tiniest hesitation. Right now she was really glad she'd shaved recently, though she was still a little insecure about her skills in bed. Not that she thought they were for sure going to end up in bed. Probably they wouldn't, she kept telling herself.

She and Doug had never been very adventurous, but not because she wasn't interested. He just had so many hangups, and she didn't want to pressure him. She thought that made her a caring lover then, but made her an inexperienced one now. She pushed that thought aside and tried to remember being in college, before Doug, when she was open and uninhibited. She reminded herself that she did know a little bit about male pleasure, and she had been told what a good kisser she was. Amazing, even. That always kind of surprised her, since the way she kissed just came naturally. Apparently, good kissing is not as common as you might think.

She pinned her confidence to those ancient compliments as Ryan led her to the elevator, which was full of people heading back to their rooms to get ready for the final gathering. As they rode up, Peach had the impression they were whispering to each other about the two of them, particularly after Ryan put his hand on the small of her back, bowed his head down to her hair and gave her a little nuzzle.

Maybe they all were realizing that the little fire episode last night was real passion, and not a show after all. Or maybe they just thought she was cheating on her pathetic husband. Either way, for the first time ever Peach was enjoying the curious expressions and lip-biting of onlookers. For so long she had tried to avoid notoriety, instead shining her light on her kids or Doug. She still wasn't sure how much attention she really wanted, but for now she was trying on the identity of not only a romance author whose book Rose Ramble had praised, but also a soft sensual goddess, widely considered among at least a dozen men to be an exceptionally good kisser, and who had the stunningly perfect Ryan Slate wrapped around her.

Something ancient and hungry was waking up inside, and she was sure that if she didn't feed it something hearty, something truly satisfying, she might never feel like a whole woman again. Maybe that was overstating things a bit—the day had been so heady and unreal, after all—but if ever there were a time to take an outsized pleasure in filling that void of desire in her life, it was now, in this moment.

They still weren't alone when they reached the top floor, but they were the only ones who got out there. Everyone else stayed on the elevator as the doors closed, and Peach and Ryan both laughed.

"I guess they wanted to see if we were getting off together," he said with an impish twinkle in his eye.

The twelfth floor looked a little different than the others—there were fewer doors on the hall, and they were double doors, while floor-to-ceiling windows at either end allowed you to gander at views of the bay and the river.

Peach and Ryan wandered slowly, leaning into each other, the fingers of their hands interlaced and gently squeezing. He led them to the last door before the window at the end of the hall, and she took a peek down, feeling like if she were to jump out, she could fly. He let go of her hand to unlock the door, and held it open for her.

"After you."

"Who says there are no more gentlemen?"

"Somebody who's never been to a romance convention?"

Peach laughed, though she was feeling a little nervous entering a man's room. A man she hardly knew—the first man outside of Doug she had even come close to getting jiggy with in over thirty years. But looking at his smiling face, and riding high on what she considered her first successful weekend of being an author, she smirked slyly and sauntered past him into the room like she belonged there. Like he was the lucky one. And she didn't even worry that she might trip.

When the door clicked closed behind her however, she felt her throat tighten a little and she swallowed hard. Peach took in the room. A wall of windows with a balcony over-looked the bay, while the lamps were set to what she would call "mood lighting." There was a large seating area with a full-size couch, two armchairs, and a couple of side tables, all in varying shades of beige punctuated with deep red accents. She spotted a door to what she assumed was the bedroom.

"Would you make me a drink? Nothing too strong." Peach needed something to help her calm the fuck down, but she also wanted to stay clear and able to make decisions.

"How about lemon club soda with a splash of vodka? Pretty sure we've got that." He peeled off his button shirt and hung it on one of the diner chairs. Peach felt her face go hot when she saw the gray tee underneath was tight on his tanned biceps.

"Sounds perfect," she said, swallowing.

"Please, have a seat." He motioned her towards the couch and headed for the kitchenette.

Peach sidled over to the couch and perched at one end. Her ass-hugging jeans had loosened over the day and were a little more comfortable than they had been this morning. She was grateful she'd brought extra freshen-up wipes, in case she felt she needed them again.

She snuck a quick text to Marny.

> Peach: I'm in his room. He's making cocktails. Wanted you to know in case I disappear.

> Marny: Enjoy the cocktails, but text me in the morning. Have fun! Be happy!

Peach tucked her phone back into her bag and pulled out the list Ryan had given her. She tried to speak but croaked instead. He looked over his shoulder at her.

"A-hem. Sorry." She waved the list. "So, my first concert ever, that my parents took us to? Or the first concert I chose to go to myself, when I was thirty-two?"

He let out a chuckle as the ice clinked into the glass. "While knowing the concerts your parents took you to tells me a lot about what they're like, I am way more curious about the latter detail. Thirty-two?"

"Afraid so. I mean I hardly went out at all in my high school years, and when I was in college money was tight. It wasn't until my kids grew up a bit and I got a weekend job at a craft store that I earned my first real spending money, and the first thing I spent it on was a concert."

"Ah," said Ryan from the minibar. "I like that."

"Yeah, Lydia and Jack were with their grandparents for a couple of weeks and Melissa hadn't come along yet, so I felt a little less guilty doing something just for myself."

He came over and leaned down to hand her the drink. She took it and looked up at him.

Here they were. Just the two of them. He winked and sat in one of the armchairs, at an angle to her and very close, so her right knee was almost touching his left. She felt warm just thinking of his knee touching hers—perfectly innocent and casual, yet somehow almost more intimate than holding hands. He took a sip of his drink, then set it on the glass side table. She took two little sips of hers and set it down next to his.

"So? I'm dying to know," Ryan said, putting his hands together and resting his elbows on his thighs, looking very relaxed but focusing all of his attention on her. With Doug, she always had to get through some barrier or other to communicate, be it football, karate class, the newspaper—there were so many things more interesting to him than she was. But everything about Ryan seemed to signal genuine interest, which was helping because she was not used to talking so much about herself. Even writing her author bio had been torture.

"Dave Matthews, 2003. I went with Marny, Jessica, Tara, and Angela. She was actually the biggest Dave Matthews fan in the group."

"Did Angela talk you into it?" Here, his knee finally made contact with hers, connecting a circuit.

"No, actually, I talked them all into it." As she spoke, Peach reached for her glass again and Ryan turned to pick up his. She noticed his chiseled arm flexing. She also felt his knee shift, pressing harder against hers, sending an electric wave through her. If he felt it, he pretended not to, so she did the same and carried on.

"I had heard the song 'Crash Into Me' before, whenever it came out, and I thought it was one of the sexiest songs I'd ever heard. I would listen to it on repeat, and I got the idea I really wanted to hear it in person. I didn't tell them that—I just said I would organize a girl's weekend around the concert. They were not hard to convince."

"Nice," appraised Ryan, nodding. "Yeah, I remember that was a very popular tour. I didn't see it, but I know Dave Matthews was hot at the time. It's been a while since I've heard that song though."

"It's on one of my regular playlists. I still love it. It never got old for me."

With a little smile, Ryan got up and headed over to the desk. He made a few taps on the tablet lying there, and music started up. She recognized it immediately as the song she had just told him about, and felt her face flush, followed by a rush of blood to various other body parts as he came back over to her.

"Would you like to dance?" He extended his hand to her. So effortless for him, but there was something so full of desire about an empty hand, palm up, hovering in front of you.

She put her hand in his and rose to him. He took her waist and she put her hands on his shoulders, first the right, then the left, feeling his body heat through the cotton of his shirt. She felt the same fluttery excitement she had as a girl, whenever a cute boy came up to her at a school dance.

Dave sang in that low whispery voice of his as the slow sensual melody played, and they swayed together, first with a little bit of air still between them. Then he pulled her in closer, taking his time. She leaned her head on his chest as they swayed and melted into the warmth between them. He smelled of freshly washed cotton, coconut, and warm dark spices. She could lean on him like this all night and it would be enough. It would be the perfect dessert to a long and lovely meal of many courses.

He started to hum the tune and she felt the vibration travel down the very center of her. As the song closed out he nuzzled the top of her head and she tucked in tighter, wanting no air between them—wanting to press every part of her to him. She felt him relax his hold and lean away a bit, so she let herself be ready to say goodnight, if that was what was about to happen.

Instead he looked down at her and put a curled finger under her chin, lifting her face to look up at his. He paused, making sure that they were on the same page, and slowly lowered his mouth to hers. She felt his hot lips and the warm salt flavor of him, and spread her fingers out over his strong shoulders, claiming him. They started slow, sensual, tender—surrendering to each other—and the more she tasted him, inhaled him, the hungrier she got, and he kept feeding her his lips, his breath and his want.

The first thing to come off was Ryan's tee. She couldn't bear to pull her mouth away from his. Their tongues danced and plundered as she helped him tug the shirt from his arms and over his head. Only then did their kisses wait as he flung it away. When she saw Ryan's bare chest—the patch of dark hair across it with a few silver hairs peppered at the center, and muscular pecs like she'd never touched before—it left her dizzy with excitement. This man half naked in her arms made her ache in a way she thought her body had long forgotten.

She let out a throaty, sexy sigh that ended with a whimper of helpless desire, and Ryan responded immediately, putting his hungry mouth to hers again as they pressed into each other. Now his hands were sliding up the back of her shirt, caressing her soft round contours. She pulled back enough to peel off her own shirt, revealing a black plunge bra that gave her full and kissable cleavage. She watched him as he watched her, and the fire in his eyes said he liked what he saw. She turned and backed against him, pressing her bottom against his hips, and his hands went to her waist, sending electricity all through her. They both were still in pants, but she could feel how hard he was. How much he wanted her.

She pulled his burly arms around her and put his hands

on her breasts to cup, moaning as he did. He kissed the side of her neck, nuzzled into her hair, nibbled gently at her ear, all while squeezing her breasts through her bra and pressing as much of himself he could against the back of her. Peach took his hands and kissed the back of each one once, then turned in his arms to face him.

"Unhook my bra," she whispered.

Their mouths found each other again, and they inhaled and kissed and pressed while he pulled her bra from her shoulders and tossed it to the side. Her naked breasts swung free and her hard nipples kissed his chest as he squeezed her as close as possible, their bare torsos pressing and moving, her soft flesh against his firmness.

A weekend of flirty exchanges had manifested in this hot, all-consuming moment. He bent forward and she put her arms around his neck as he scooped her up in a hug that lifted her feet off the floor. He carried her into the bedroom and didn't bother to close the door.

Ryan had somehow lit candles, which were flickering on the side table, along with a bottle of champagne on ice and a box of chocolates on the bed with rose petals around it. She hadn't noticed any of those romantic gestures because this man was filling up every sense she had at the moment and it enveloped her wholly. From somewhere came the thought that she hoped he was having as much fun as she was, but even that concern was a distant one, because right now she was putting her pleasure, her desire, her want first. She figured any man worth a damn would want it that way.

Setting her next to the bed, he allowed some space between them so he could make a show of taking off his jeans. She watched him in the flickering candles, the lights of Baltimore off in the distance, and felt like she was in a movie scene. His fingers popped the button and he slowly unzipped, watching her expression with great pleasure as she gave him a devilish grin. He pushed down the jeans revealing a very tight pair of black underwear that was struggling to hold his hard cock in. She could see the line of it going all the way up to the waistband, the tip almost peeking out. The desire to reach out and put her finger to it washed over her, but that had to wait a moment while she unzipped her jeans and stepped out of them. She knew her peach-colored lace panties weren't hiding much—she was all but naked before him, and she felt sexy as hell because he was looking at her like a hungry wolf about to pounce on a tasty little rabbit.

He then slipped his thumbs into the waistband of his boxer briefs and watched Peach's face as he lowered them. His long erection sprung free and all Peach was thinking was that she couldn't wait to sit on it. She loved being on top but hadn't been for years, and though the size of him might be a little bit of a challenge, it was one she was up for.

"You are so fucking sexy," she purred.

"Thank you, so are you," he said in a smooth low voice, and kicked the briefs aside.

She took in the whole sight of him, standing there with candlelight kissing his body, his pecs, his strong shoulders, his salt and pepper hair, slightly wavy tonight. His breathing got deeper as he stood there and let her look, and her eyes traveled on down the length of him—his six-pack, the sexy trail of hair that led to his cock, those strong thighs and calves. She imagined he did some lifting, because damn.

"My turn," she said. "Why don't you help me?"

He got a twinkle in his eyes and kneeled in front of her, which she wasn't expecting. Even kneeling he was tall, and he wrapped his hands around her hips, strong fingers sinking into velvet flesh. He put his mouth to her plush tummy and for a moment she thought about all of the stretch marks from three pregnancies—a thought that flitted completely away when he began peppering her belly with kisses.

He then slipped his fingers under the waistband of her lacy panties and slid them down over her curves and dimples in one smooth, seductive movement, his hands embracing her all along the way. "Mmm," Peach breathed and stepped out of them, and he tossed the panties aside and took a look at her soft downy mound.

Another flicker of self-doubt—she had never been one to wax or shave there. She didn't have a lot to begin with, and it felt silly to keep up with something that didn't matter to her. Now it mattered, and she was a little worried he was expecting her to be waxed like a model—not that there was anything she could do about it at the moment. This was how she was made, and she really didn't feel like there was anything wrong with it, so she decided if he wanted to fuck her bad enough, a little bit of womanly hair wouldn't dissuade him.

And it didn't. He put his broad hands around her hips, squeezing her ass and burying his nose into the velvety soft-ness. Peach's every nerve ending was on high alert, her body tingling and pulsing all over. The smells of his shampoo, his soap and cologne rose up to her—a special Ryan blend that was new and exciting, and one she would now always recognize. As he nuzzled her he made a humming sound that sent vibrations between her legs and made her pulse even more intensely.

Breathing heavily, with gooseflesh all over, she curled her fingers around his upper arms and gently tugged him back to his feet. She took his hand and led him over to the bed, where she perched on the end and let her legs spread apart.

She grabbed his hips and pulled him closer, first kissing one hipbone, then the other. She caressed the planes of his hips surrounding his cock and smiled when it jumped a little. She put a hand at the base of his cock and kissed the tip, then took in as much as she could. He gasped and stroked his fingertips along her upper arms, and the skin contact left a buzz everywhere he touched her.

She worked his cock with her hand and mouth, kissing and caressing him as if she'd been doing it her whole life. She wasn't thinking about technique—she was so hungry for it, enjoying it so much, she could feel his pleasure mounting.

With a few final kisses she released him and scooted back onto the bed, her thighs relaxed and open for a good view. She scooped up some of the scattered rose petals and sprinkled them onto her belly. Sprinkled a few more onto her soft mound. Peach invited him between her legs with her eyes and he climbed onto the bed and covered her body with his. There was so much she wanted to do with him—every sexy thing she had ever imagined—but her desire had reached a frenzy and she only wanted him inside of her, this second.

"Fuck me. Now," she said, low and smooth and certain.

He reached into the bed table, took out a little packet and tore it open with his teeth. Ryan rolled the condom down and settled into her again, pressing the tip of his cock to the center of her split. He pushed gently in, a little at a time, while he lowered his mouth to hers and kissed her. As he pushed in deeper, a circuit of electric lust and passion pulsed through them.

"Yes! Oh my god yes!" Peach couldn't stay quiet. She was by nature a bit of a talker, but usually she suppressed it because there was something a little embarrassing about it. Especially with a passionless lover. But tonight, with this beautiful man, she was all in, and she let loose with abandon, moaning and panting and talking as he moved with her. She watched him above, his arms flexing, his collarbone prominent, his handsome face overcome with pleasure. Then she would close her eyes, relishing the sensation of him filling her up and hitting her so deep, until she started to let out screams of passion, not giving a damn that someone might hear her.

Ryan was holding her so close now, every part of his body moving with hers, his breath in her ear softly saying, "Peach, oh, Peach!" and in one last deep thrust he quaked and pulsed inside her. He held her through that final ecstatic moment, then he was kissing her sweaty neck, kissing her cheek and her forehead, smelling her hair and saying her name before collapsing beside her.

She hated the feeling of him pulling out his cock. They had been so close, so plugged into each other, she wanted to just keep him there inside her. She smiled softly and rolled over to look at his spent body, still so powerful, tanned and glistening. His face looked so peaceful and boyish. She went up on her hands and leaned in to kiss his chin.

He let out a small exhausted laugh. "Thank you, milady."

She'd never been called that before, so she played along with his silliness.

"Thank *you*, my lord."

He reached across and stroked her arm.

"That was amazing. How are you doing?"

"Amazing. The only thing is …" she hesitated, not wanting to sound like this was anything less than spectacular.

"Is …?" he prompted, clearly wanting to know.

Ah, what the hell. "That I didn't get to be on top. That's my favorite. Or it used to be—I haven't done it in so long."

He rolled onto his side and leaned up on his elbow, his head in his hand.

"Well, there *must* be *something* we can do about that."

Peach giggled. "There *must* be."

Peach peeled a few rose petals off of her thighs, reached over the side of the bed and let them flit to the floor. She saw the chocolate box at the corner of the bed. Somehow it had survived the thrashing, and she popped it open.

"Oh boy, a little mix," she delighted.

"Yes, I had no idea what your favorites were, so I used the shotgun approach."

She reached in and picked up what looked like a cherry cordial and held it to his mouth. He bit carefully into it, some of the liquid running down his chin anyway.

"Oops," they said together.

She lidded the box and put it on the nightstand and then leaned in to lick the sweet syrup from his chin, which had just the slightest scratch of stubble.

This led to a lot of rolling around, kissing and exploring each other. Their lips and hands found some of each other's most sensitive places, and soon both of them were aroused and hungry all over again. This time Peach reached into the drawer to pull out a condom, and wondered for a moment if this was just part of Ryan's careful preparation for the evening or if he routinely kept a box of them on hand. She decided it didn't matter, as she pulled the condom down his long hard cock. Finally she climbed on top, and let Ryan enjoy her full-throated ecstasy. Together they did all of the things she had wanted to do for so many years, and she didn't feel one bit selfish or self-conscious about it, because the moans and cries that Ryan made only confirmed that she was giving as good as she got.

Two hours later they finally collapsed, utterly spent.

They ate more chocolate, sipped champagne, and talked quietly until words stopped having meaning and their brains grew fuzzy. Legs tangled, a single sheet draped across them, Peach nestled down under Ryan's arm and fell asleep to the rising and falling of his chest and the beating of his heart, and it all felt so right and essential.

THE NEXT MORNING Peach woke up alone and a bit disoriented. Where was Ryan? She rolled over and squinted at her phone. It was after nine and she could make out there were half a dozen text messages from Marny. Still blinky-eyed from sleep, she recorded a voice-to-text message:

> Just woke up. I'm alive and way okay. Will tell you more later. Love ya.

She had a moment of panic that Ryan had done a wham-bam-thank-you-ma'am, but she rethought all that when she logicked out that she was in his room and clearly all his stuff was still there. Maybe he hoped she would skedaddle before he got back, though she had no idea what the current one-night stand etiquette was, so she figured she'd oblige.

She stood up, wrapping the sheet around her naked body, and walked over to gaze out at the Chesapeake Bay. She'd just had one of the best weekends of her life and whatever came next, even if it was a bit of a letdown, she would always feel grateful for the experience. She'd leave a lovely note for Ryan and head back to her room to pack. She sauntered to the bathroom and took a quick shower, then slid on her panties and peeked out the bedroom door to see if she could locate her bra and shirt and shoes.

He still wasn't anywhere in sight. Already she was feeling post-performance anxiety, imagining how she compared to the models he must have slept with, younger women with more creative skills and stamina. Even in college she would compare herself like that, and it always ended in a downward spiral. But this was the new Peach, the Second Book in the Series Peach, Peach the wanton sex goddess, so she stopped that line of thinking in its tracks and told herself that they both had fun, and that was enough. She grabbed her shirt and pulled it on.

The door to the suite beeped and swung open and Ryan came in, dressed in workout clothes and smiling, a big bouquet of flowers in his hands.

"Good morning sunshine," he said.

"Hey."

She was a little startled, but prepared to be gently ushered out. God, he did look fantastic though, in his tight tank and running shorts, all muscled and strong.

She felt very exposed in the harsh daylight rays, wearing only her top and panties and not in the throes of passion. As if she were on display and every bump, sag, wrinkle, and ripple was highlighted, and she tugged at the hem of the shirt to try and edge it down over her dimpled bottom and thighs.

Ok, this confident goddess stuff clearly isn't going to happen all in one day, she said to herself.

"Breakfast will be up in a few minutes. I took the liberty of ordering something for you. Hope that's okay?"

Breakfast? She wondered if it would be plain oatmeal, berries and yogurt. So many people passive-aggressively serve plus-sized women the food they considered healthier, "for their own good."

"Oh, I thought you … um, I thought you left so I could head out without you having to … you know." She sidled over to the chair and scooped up her pants and slid them on carefully so she didn't finish the weekend off by falling on her butt in front of him, with that being the last klutzy thing he remembers about her. She'd prefer he remember the mind-blowing sex goddess from last night.

He furrowed his brows slightly. "To … what?"

"To like, deal with me. We had fun and that's that." She turned away and lifted up her shirt and put her bra on and pulled the shirt back down. She felt less vulnerable now, even though all her makeup had washed off and she probably looked like a drowned cat. When she turned back around she saw a look of concern had washed over his face.

"Is that how you feel?"

"Me? Well … no, but I figured you …" she did kind of half shrug.

He watched her face and waited for more, slightly narrowing his eyes. He wasn't making this easy.

"Well, I just figured you might have more interesting things to do with your time than hang out with me."

"Sounds like you didn't see my note," he said, and laid the flowers on the little dining table. He walked into the bedroom and plucked a piece of paper off the nightstand.

She knitted her brows as he handed her the note:

Peach,

Thank you for a fantastic evening. You are a wonder! I have to do my workout, then I'll be back and have breakfast with you if you have time. I get *another answer from the list today, right? Relax and enjoy the room. Let's do something fun today if you don't have to head back to Pennsylvania.*

Ryan

Peach shook her head and made a crooked little smile as she let the words "fantastic evening" engrave themselves in her memory. She had given Ryan a fantastic evening. Amazing. She could not wait to tell Marny everything.

"Oh, Ryan. I seem to be an idiot. I just assumed …"

"I am starting to feel like you think I'm a bit of a cad."

"Well, to be honest the thought had crossed my mind. Hot model? Big box of condoms? Convention circuit with a lot of romance-minded women? Sorry, that does sound kind of judgy. But I think more than that, what this is, is about me not feeling like you could actually want me. It's still hard to believe, even after last night. There's a lot of years of conditioning behind that. It probably won't go away anytime soon. So if it's annoying then you're probably going to find yourself frustrated with me. I'm frustrated with me."

She paused in case he needed to say she was right, but he didn't, so she continued.

"I'm glad I'm at least old enough to be able to articulate these feelings. Anyway, I think it would maybe be better to just remember the amazing night we had and leave it at that."

When that came out of her mouth she felt a pang. She didn't want him to agree with that. She didn't want to leave this room, for at least the next week. She was saying what she thought she should say, not what she actually wanted to say, which was *Let's go have a picnic somewhere we can fuck like bunnies by a stream because I want to see you naked in the sunshine and feel our sweat slick between us as we move on a blanket while the sky watches.*

He moved in closer to her, slowly, considerately.

"I'd like to give you a hug." He opened his arms.

Without hesitation she walked right into them and wrapped her arms around his waist and buried her face in his chest. He was still a little damp from working out and he smelled of his sun-warmed skin and tropical-scented sunblock. She hung in that moment and thought of nothing else but the beats of their hearts.

"If it helps, I bought the condoms yesterday. In case you wanted to come dance with me." He kissed the top of her forehead and gently released her, went over to the small dining table and picked up the flowers.

"I got these for you. There are a dozen different kinds here, I was hoping one of them might be your favorite. We hadn't gotten to that on the list yet."

She got a little choked up at this gesture, and her eyes went soft and welled up a bit. She took the flowers from him and held them to her chest. Gave them a sniff and examined them. She smiled over the bouquet and pointed.

"This one. Tiger lily."

"Ha! I really thought it would take two or three bouquets before I figured it out. So, pink? Like this one?"

"I like the orange ones. Or I did." She twirled the bloom between her fingers and smelled it. "Tiger lilies will always have a special place in my heart. Doug used to bring them to me, when we were young. And then later, when he wanted to apologize."

She gave Ryan a thank-you kiss on the cheek. She could feel her spirit glowing.

"But I'm done with Doug. And with tiger lilies. I'm

ready for something different. When I figure out what my next favorite flower is, you'll be the first to know, promise."

Something crossed Ryan's normally tranquil expression. It looked to her like concern.

"You're not leaving your husband for me are you? That's not something I want to be responsible for."

Now Peach had a rush of uncomfortable energy wash over her.

"Wait, you knew I was married. I mentioned it the other night. Were you only getting involved with me *because* I'm married? An easy out? No commitment?"

"Again, the assumption that I'm a cad."

"I think the more recent term is 'player'."

"Look, I like you. I actually like you a lot. But this is who I am. When I meet a woman who is having a bit of a waver in her confidence I can't help but want to make her feel better. Build up her confidence, make her feel special. Because they *are* special. Is that a bad thing?"

"I don't suppose it would be, if you had laid your cards on the table at the beginning. Ooh, Ryan! You really are good at this game. You sure had me going. I thought you liked me."

"I do like you! Peach, I'm sorry, you're right. I should have been clearer. But all this isn't about me getting laid, or playing games. I just wanted you to see yourself as beautiful, to help you feel better about yourself. But not if that makes me a homewrecker."

Peach snatched her shoes, phone and purse and marched past Ryan, who watched her pass without saying a word. She turned at the door.

"I wish I had just left before you got back from your workout."

She opened the big double door just as room service was

delivering a cart full of waffles, bacon, sausage, coffee, orange juice, fruit, the works. She grunted and went past the clerk and stomped off to her room in her bare feet, feeling like a complete idiot.

First she had a good cry, then dug a six-dollar bottle of orange juice out of the fridge and drank it down, and finally called Marny and told her everything.

"I do not think you're an idiot. Clearly he knows what he's doing, and right up until that moment happened, you were very happy. You still had a great weekend. Just try to forget that very last part."

"The energy we had together felt so good. So real. I can't trust that feeling ever again."

"He didn't say he didn't like you. In fact he said he did like you. A bunch of times. Right? I think your emotions and hormones are all dusted up. Get your stuff packed up and then when you get here I'll be waiting at the airport and we can take another little trip for apps and margs. Okay?"

Peach sniffed as her tears were finally to a trickle. "Ok, Marn. Thanks."

"Sweetie, it's been a hell of a week for you."

"You got that right. Bye. Love you."

"Love you, too. Bye."

TWELVE

Viral

Marny was there with sympathy and a smile when Peach dragged her sad sorry ass through the gate. They collected her bags and got into Marny's car and only then did Peach realize she didn't know where she was going. She hadn't communicated with Doug about who would be at the house and when—for all she knew he was home from Lenny's and back with Tara, recreating the scene from earlier in the week with his stupid socks on. God, was that just last Tuesday?

She dug out the credit card Doug had given her for emergencies. She figured this qualified—at least to her it did, and if he didn't think so he could fuck all the way off. She booked a hotel room online not too far from the airport, and she and Marny roared off.

After lugging her stuff up to the room, they discovered the hotel had a loungey little bar that was pretty empty. She and Marny settled in a dark corner booth and drank white wine and ate artichoke dip while Peach told her all of the good parts of the weekend. Only the good parts, Marny had said, and if Peach strayed from that rule she would put up a skinny little finger and wag it at her.

"Wow. So Rose Ramble doesn't just like your book, she thought it was so good, she made sure you were there! And she made sure to tell you about it, and she said, 'Keep writing.' And while I'm not at all surprised, I will say that I did tell you it was good. This is my I-told-you-so face, in case you missed it."

Peach laughed and bumped her head against Marny's. "You're right. There was a lot of great stuff that happened this weekend." She sighed and took another long sip. Her phone rang a familiar tune. "I need to grab it. It's Melissa."

"Tell her I said hello," Marny said, and waived the server down for two more glasses of wine.

Peach's side of the conversation went, "Hello honey! Yes, I did. Yes. She … who? What did she do? I did sell some this weekend, but I didn't think anybody would have read it already. Okay, I won't. I promise I won't. Yes, okay. Love you. Bye."

Marny scrutinized Peach's expression, which read a little like shock to her, if she had to guess.

"Now what?" Marny asked.

"Melissa has some kind of notification set up for if my name comes up online somewhere. And she wanted to tell me that my name came up somewhere."

"The face you're making is telling me it's not a good thing."

"I don't know. It doesn't sound great. She said it's viral, but I don't really have a grasp of the scope of it. Some book reviewer on social media apparently said some rather critical things about my book in a video."

"Well, that's good right? Reviews are a normal part of the book thing."

"She made me promise not to get upset and give up writing."

"Oh boy. Well did she say where to find this review?"

"She said just put my name into a search engine and it would come up."

Marny hesitated, but finally tapped "Peach Kincaid" into the search bar and several results came up, including the video of her being rescued by Ryan, which Marny intended to watch to the end later. But the rest led to a video that was a three-minute review of her book *Greyson Edging*.

"I bet it's that twenty-year-old who was wearing the blinged out Book Slut shirt. Shit, what was her name?"

"Book slut?" Marny screwed up her face.

"It looks like it's TouchingMyShelf_Reads on TikTok. Apparently you don't have to have the app to see it. Hold on." Marny clicked a few links and eventually found the video. "Okay, got it. Are you ready?" She looked at Peach to assess her lack of apprehension, which suggested a certain amount of social media innocence that Marny was pretty sure was about to be shattered.

Peach nodded resolutely. "I'm ready."

The video opened with the reviewer, who Peach recognized as one of the people who bought her book. She was in her late twenties, with a brassy bleached bowl cut and a long pinched face, wearing a blue sweater vest and glasses in what seemed to be a very forced academic aesthetic. She stood in front of a bookshelf with lots of figurines and flowers and other things one might presume had something to do with the stories in the books. Miss TouchingMyShelf held up a copy of Peach's book and showed off her plaid nails clicking the cover.

"All of us bookish romance lovers want to find our newest

author addiction. I found this book by an unknown author at Rambling Romanticon this past weekend hoping she would be what I was dreaming of so I could send you her way to blaze a trail through this app. As all of you know I can put away a book in four or five hours if I want, and this one was easy as it's only 60k words, so it only took me about three hours and it was three hours too long. Why you being so mean Andi, you ask? I'm not, it's just my opinion. I'm sure this book is right for somebody, but it is a hard pass for me. The characters were boring and old—I don't think there was anybody under forty. I can't even imagine who the market for this book is. I'm shocked the author even knew what 'edging' means, she looked like some Midwest cookie-baking nana who accidentally dropped into the convention. Even she seemed surprised to be there—she didn't have any swag and her display was seriously lacking."

"Ouch," Marny said. Peach shushed her.

"Books you could try instead—" and here Andi did some flips and movements that transitioned into other books that weren't remotely comparable to Peach's. "You can buy these books through the links in my bio. If you were at Rambling Romanticon in Maryland this weekend reshare this with your hot takes from the event. Don't forget, like, follow, share, repost!"

"Why would this be viral?" Marny mused. "I mean it has about six thousand views, which is a lot, but not nearly what qualifies as viral."

She knew a bit more about social media than Peach. For instance, she knew the video they saw, though snarky and pandering, didn't seem like anything special. She clicked into the comments and found many people were defending Peach, which was kind of comforting. Then they both saw it.

Comment from BookLoreQueenReading: "Crying after I saw the video comment from RomanceConGoer4eva just go to her account to see it. I would die."

"I don't understand, Marn."

"I think it's the response video to this video that might have gone viral. We better go look at it."

"Oh god." Peach didn't like the sound of that.

"Andi has about eight thousand followers, looks like RomanceConGoer4eva has about twenty-five thousand followers. Goodness. Okay, let me see if I can find it." It didn't take long since it was just two posts back. "These people do not waste time getting content up."

"I guess not."

"Brace yourself," Marny said.

She clicked on the video and it showed a snippet of Andi's video, then a different woman came on the screen, whom Peach also recognized, though she hadn't bought her book.

"Friends, I was at Rambling Romaticon this weekend and at first I did not put two-and-two together. I am sorry, but I have got to share." A backdrop behind her changed to what appeared to be a group of people, the image seemed to be frozen video. "I was recording Rebecca Jazz, a cover model on like fifty romance covers, on our plane after it landed, and caught this."

"Oh Jesus no," Peach groaned.
Marny paused the video. "What?"

Peach's face grew hot and flush and she sank way down in her seat. Marny pushed play.

RomanceConGoer4eva pointed at the video still. "That's Peach Kincaid on the same plane as we are, about to get off," and she leaned aside to let the video play out behind her.

Marny squinted at the screen in dread.

RomanceConGoer4eva giggled. "Sound up!" A robust fart sound followed. Then she burst out laughing. "I heard she had a full-on blowout and had to run off of the plane and change."

Marny turned a little green. She clicked on the view counter and saw that the video had over two million views. Peach gulped down her wine and laid down on the booth seat.

"Please just push me off the highest bridge you can find."

"I wanted to say it wasn't that bad to make you feel better, but damn."

Marny waved over the server and asked for a bottle of Prosecco to take up to Peach's room. She managed to convince her that nobody in the hotel had any idea there was a viral romance book world drama unfolding, or that she was at the center of it, in order to pry her out of the booth. They skulked off to the room where Peach stepped into the shower and washed off the day, wishing she could wash off so much more. She sat on the edge of the bed, hair dripping, shivering from the blasting AC, totally walleyed.

"What the hell was I thinking going to that convention

this weekend?" Peach's voice was flat and emotionless. "This is my own fault for doing something for myself. See? See what happens when you're selfish and indulge in crazy fantasies?"

"Well, up until the moment that it went south with Ryan, it was going pretty well."

"I can never show my face in public again. I certainly can't ever go to another romance convention. Not even to buy books. All of those people will have seen this and heard about it."

Peach was shivering harder.

"I wish I could say that woman's critique of my book was more embarrassing, but that plane video has done me in. I was so embarrassed that day, but I had convinced myself that I didn't know any of those people and I'd never see any of them ever again."

Marny walked over to the suitcase and found a long black tee and pulled it over Peach's head. Peach stood up and let it slip to mid thigh. She threw the damp towel in a corner, crawled into the bed and curled up, shivering.

"Tara is going to see that video. Doug is going to see that video." Then she made a gasp and sobbed out, "Ryan is going to see that video!"

Marny perched on the end of the bed and rubbed Peach's back.

"Sweetie, it's just a little passed gas. It's normal, and although embarrassing, everybody does it. Some people aren't even the slightest bit embarrassed by stuff like that. Maybe you could pretend to be one of those people."

Then Peach stopped shaking and sat herself up, her brows knit.

"Wait, play it again."

Marny gave her an uncertain look but pulled up the video and hit play. Peach watched over her shoulder.

"Mother. Fucker," she said with a vengeful tone.

"What?" Marny played the grainy snippet again.

"That's like altered or something." She jabbed her finger at the phone. "Those aren't the people who were near me, I know exactly who was near me. And yes, that's my head, but look. Peach hit the back arrow until she came to one of the videos from the fire when Ryan carried her out of the ballroom.

"First of all that fart sound is way too loud. It was a little squeak, I'm telling you! Second of all it's a slightly different angle, but this image of me looks like it's from the ballroom. Look, you can see a tiny bit of my shoulder, my bare shoulder. I had a tee on in the plane. This video is a fake!"

"Wait, are you sure?" Marny replayed it a couple of times and compared it to the ballroom video. "Oh my god. Why would that chick do that?"

"I don't know, but it's seriously fucked up. Show me how to put that app on my phone."

THIRTEEN

Liars and Cheats

Four days later Peach met Doug at Nickle Plated, a diner where they used to go whenever they had a free Sunday so Peach could eat pancakes she didn't have to make. They would chat about the week they'd had, make plans for the one coming up—typical married people stuff. It was something Peach particularly liked because someone brought her food and she didn't have to do dishes and it made her happy to push open the door to the cool AC and the smell of bacon.

She intentionally got there a bit ahead of him so she could settle in before having to have a serious talk about the house and the divorce. It seemed a little rash to be talking divorce before they even gave therapy a chance, but Peach simply didn't have it in her to rehash all the things that had gone wrong. More than that, she didn't have the patience to wait and see if Doug was finally going to make himself a better partner for her. She felt totally done.

She ordered the fresh fruit cup, protein pancakes with whipped cream, and extra crispy bacon. She sipped on coffee until Doug arrived, five minutes late and wearing wrinkled clothes and an expression that she thought was one of sad acceptance.

"You look a little better than last time I saw you," she said. The server dropped off her breakfast.

"Can I get you anything, sir?" the young woman asked.

"Just coffee and one of your big cinnamon rolls. Thanks."

"I'll be back shortly," she said and headed off towards the bakery case and coffee pots.

Doug slid in the other side of the booth.

"Yeah, I still don't have the hang of the laundry yet, but at least I showered and shaved. When you saw me I was a real wreck."

"Yeah," Peach said, slicing off a piece of pancake with her fork and taking a perfectly sized bite, followed by a sip of her well creamed and sugared coffee.

"I'm sorry about everything, Peach. We'll do this however you want to do it."

Peach took another bite and then followed it with some strawberry. She nodded and eyeballed him as she sipped again.

"And maybe I shouldn't mention it, but I'm sorry about that video all over the internet. I know that's a touchy subject for you. You must be ready to hide under a rug."

He seemed sincere enough, but it was hard to trust a man who cheated on her like that. It colored anything he said.

"Thanks, but the video is a fake."

He looked like he didn't believe it.

"It's a fake, Doug, yes."

"Okay, why would somebody do that? It seemed real enough."

"Who knows? All anybody thinks about is going viral so

they can get some money. I don't know why she did it, or where she got the video from, but I am going to find out."

"But you don't really know much about the internet and social media stuff."

"No, I don't. But a few years ago I didn't know how to write and publish a book either, and I did that."

"You sure did. I'm proud —"

"Don't," she said, and pushed a large manila envelope towards him. "My lawyer drew this up yesterday. It's very basic. Even split on everything." She took a sip of water and watched him.

"Okay, wow. That was fast. You don't even want to try counseling first?"

"Doug, neither of us is happy. Let's take the time we have left to find ourselves."

Doug's expression turned sour and he wagged his finger in an accusatory way.

"This is because of that Romanticon firefighter guy isn't it? I saw the stuff online. The video of him carrying you out of the ballroom. What did you do after he took you out of the ballroom, Peach? Hmm?"

Peach sighed and set down her fork and took a sip of her water. "Are you really asking me that, Doug? You left, remember? The note is right there in the documentation," she pointed at a photocopy of his note when he left the house, with some of the crumple marks still visible.

He sighed and slumped in the booth seat. "I didn't know what I was saying. It was like I was drugged up or something."

"This is better for us. If you really love me you'll sign it, because it's better for *me* Doug."

Doug fingered the end of the envelope and papers. "What about the house?"

"We sell it and split the—"

"But the kids grew up in that house! Bubbles and Mittens are both buried in the backyard."

"Maybe you should have thought of that before you fucked my best friend, in our bedroom, on our anniversary sheets!" Her voice was getting louder and Doug shushed her and turned beet red.

"Alright, alright! I'm sorry. I'm sorry, Peach. It's a lot all at once."

"Yeah, no shit." She wasn't hiding her sarcasm in the least at this point. "And you'd better hope my blood test comes out negative too."

He let out a long breath and pursed his lips for a moment as if he were trying to stop himself from saying anything else stupid. He gave a small nod and pulled a pen out of his pocket, flipped a few of the pages back and signed them on the dotted line.

"Thank you." Peach felt an immense weight lifted from her. She imagined she instantly looked more peaceful.

The waitress set down Doug's roll and coffee, but he dropped a ten on the table and stood up to go.

"Bye, Peach. I'm sorry I messed things up."

She nodded and watched him walk away and out the door. She finished her breakfast slowly as she scrolled her phone for apartment rentals.

FOURTEEN

The Chesapeake Bay

Peach headed for Main Street to wait for Marny at their favorite coffee shop. The day was sunny with big fluffy clouds and the two large pots in front of the shop had colorful blooms popping up. The brick sidewalk was swept clean.

She stood there looking at her reflection in the window just as she had a couple of weeks before, and she'd have sworn she looked like a different person. She sure felt different. Hair neatly styled, makeup just so, pants with a zipper, and a low-cut body-hugging black tee. She felt very put together. She even went and got a nail touch-up a few blocks over, and chose black and pink alternating.

She felt sassy as fuck.

And she had splurged on a beautiful bright pink laptop bag and a new laptop to write on, and she now carried it with her everywhere, just in case she felt like putting down some words. She still wondered if maybe she wasn't an actual author, but she was going to do everything real authors do until she felt like one. Marny walked up behind her.

"Hey good lookin'."

Peach turned and smiled and hugged her friend.

"Oh Marn, it's so good to see you. Sorry I haven't been texting back as much as I should, I've just been overwhelmed."

"It's okay love. I understand. Been a bit busy myself ever since I stretched my region a bit into the Pittsburgh area. I sold two houses this week!"

"Oh my god, that's great! Chocolate croissant and a drink?" Peach offered.

"Let's do it."

They headed into Café Faraway and Marny held down their little nook in the front window, while Peach left her bag and went back to the counter to order lattes and croissants. When she turned to walk back to the table she saw such a look on Marny's face. Her eyes were kind of bugged out and she had a weird tight smile. Peach moved around the post and saw what she was looking at. It was Tara. She hadn't noticed Peach approaching from her flank, and Peach just froze.

Tara was making big hand motions like she was trying to tell Marny some dramatic story, with hands at her chest, then flopping forward, then back to her chest, over and over. Peach read her body language as: *What I'm saying is sad and important and you should feel bad for me.* She inched in a bit closer.

"And I swear I didn't mean for it to be like this," Tara was saying. "Peach was such a good friend and I just don't even know why I did that. We had been flirting for like four years, but only just started … you know … last year. I really didn't mean any disrespect. It wasn't about Peach."

Peach stepped up and cleared her throat. Tara stopped, turned to see her, and all of the blood drained from her face. It took a moment before she regained the ability to speak.

"I'm so sorry Peach. I'm really so sorry."

"Tara, I'll forgive you if you just answer one question."

Tara's eyes looked like they might well up, but her face stayed smooth and wrinkle-free.

"Of course, what?"

"What is your favorite flower?"

Her eyes shifted back and forth. "Um … yellow roses. Why?"

"Uh-huh." Peach said. She slid into the seat next to Marny and they both stared at Tara, who was starting to sweat in her ugly brown sundress with giant bows on the shoulders. Peach even thought her hair was starting to frizz.

"So, Tara, the yellow roses that were on my ex-husband's Facebook page just a few weeks ago, were those some kind of secret signal of love and admiration to you?"

Tara looked at the women, shifting her eyes from one to the other. She started fidgeting, her fingers sort of pinching at each other. Then she nodded.

"Well, Peach, yes. I suppose it was."

Peach also nodded, briefly, and slid her chocolate croissant out of its bag. She pinched off the end and took a bite.

"Okay, Tara, one more question, yes?"

"Okay."

"You said you didn't mean to be disrespectful, but were you disrespectful?"

Tara licked her lips in thought, then bit her lip. Finally she said, "I was disrespectful Peach, please forgive me."

Peach took a sip of her chai latte. "Okay, I forgive you Tara."

Tara breathed a sigh of relief.

"Thank you, Peach!"

"Now, I don't ever want to talk to you again. Understand?"

The smile fell from Tara's face. Her chin started to quiver and she took off out the door.

Marny let out a howl and a long laugh and smacked the table

"Holy shit, Peach! Damn!"

Other patrons who'd somehow missed the scene with Tara were now turning to look at Marny's less than subtle expression of admiration. Peach smiled and popped another bite of croissant into her mouth and chased it with more chai latte.

"I wish I could say I feel a lot better, but at least I have a little closure."

"Amen girl! Okay, now what?"

"Well I have some big news, that I was hoping you could help me with."

Marny sipped her drink with a mischievous expression and then—as delicate and ladylike as she looked in her crochet cotton tank top and sparkling accessories—she managed to stuff half a croissant in her mouth and then grinned around it impudently. There was a dab of chocolate on her nose as she muffled, "Need more fashion advice? Because damn you're killing it right now."

"I need real estate help."

Marny wiped her face and said, "Oh, right. You want me to list the house. That neighborhood is fantastic. You've had that house what, twenty-five years?"

"Twenty-three. It's nearly paid off."

"Shazam! Well, let me go do an assessment. I know some of it needs updates, but I have guys for that. Want to do it today?"

"Yeah, sure." She gave her friend a soft smile and put

her hand on Marny's. "And, I need help finding a condo. In Virginia Beach."

Marny gave her a curious look. "Like an investment property? That's a good idea. You could bring in passive income while you write."

"No Marn, I'm moving."

"What!" She dropped her pastry and pushed aside everything in front of her and turned to look Peach in the eyes. "Why? No, no, you can't move Peachy! I would miss you too much!"

Peach inhaled deeply and closed her eyes. She let it out slow and long, then opened her eyes and again put her hands on her friend's hands.

"Marny, I'm already nervous about this, so please help me. I need to do this."

"Why Virginia Beach?"

"I can't live here. Everywhere I look reminds me of the old Peach. Of Doug, and Tara. Of a different life. My cousin Lexy lives in Virginia Beach and she loves it. She was in the Navy for twenty years and retired there."

Marny nodded and squeezed Peach's hands. Peach could tell she was swallowing back tears.

"I want a condo where I can look out over the Chesapeake Bay. I've always wanted to live near the ocean. But more than that, I want to look out at the bay and think of my wonderful weekend near Baltimore when my life changed for the better. I felt like a butterfly coming out of her chrysalis. When I saw Doug with Tara I thought it was one of the worst things that had ever happened to me, but it woke me the fuck up."

"Why not Baltimore? The real estate might be a bit more affordable?"

"Because I want a beach life, with sand and summers

writing on a balcony watching people fall in love on the boardwalk. I want to smell the salt air when I wake up, and I think I want a dog to keep me company."

Marny nodded. "Of course I'll help you, friend." She let go of Peach's hands and relaxed her body a bit. "Have you heard from Slate?"

Peach looked down at the table and picked at the corner of the pastry bag.

"No. But I did ask him to give me space to think. He didn't argue. I'm probably too much work." She let out a brief bitter laugh. "He probably saw that awful fake video of me and wouldn't ever want to be seen with me again."

"Have you figured out how and why that girl did that video?"

"Not yet, but Melissa and her roommate are working on it."

"Is Ryan Slate even his real name?"

Peach thought about it for a moment. "I don't actually know. I think it is, but you're right, it does kind of sound like a stage name. I don't really know much about him now that I think about it. That's so funny."

"What?"

"That I have such big feelings for somebody I barely know."

"It's not so unusual."

"I know, but it still is kind of funny. Guess if we do get back in touch I'll have a list of questions for him, too."

"Him *too*?"

"Yeah, he gave me this list of questions about me he wanted me to answer the last day of the convention." Peach slid it out of her bag and laid it on the table in front of them.

"You just happen to have this with you?" Marny let out an amused giggle.

Peach gave a sheepish shrug. Marny took a moment to read it, and she was invested.

"This list is the most romantic thing I've ever seen in my life." She slid it back over to Peach. "No wonder you went all squishy around that man. Plus, he's so damn hot."

She licked a thumb and put it to her thigh and made a sizzle sound. Peach let out a snort and put the list back in her bag, lovingly.

"You've got it bad, girl." Marny said and tipped back her mocha latte.

"I know. Now let me tell you about some of the condos I found. I want a three bedroom. I need a bedroom, writing room, and a guest room, because you're going to come visit me all the time."

"Deal. Now let me see that list."

FIFTEEN

Angel, Ironically

Within two days the house had found a buyer. Marny was right, their neighborhood was a very desirable community, with its established trees, schools within walking distance, and attractive, well maintained properties. Peach was grateful she didn't have to endure a long drawn-out housing market drama while languishing in a hotel for months. The only tricky part was getting hers and Melissa's things packed up so quickly.

Nine days after that Peach was in Virginia Beach with Marny touring condos on the Chesapeake Bay side of town. She had begun looking at units that were a couple of blocks in from shore—a good bit cheaper, but where she could still feel the salt air—though Marny hadn't given up on finding something closer to the water.

Peach couldn't believe how fast everything was going forward, but Marny said having a large chunk of cash from the sale of the house moved the financing along very quickly. It also helped that Peach's name had been on the mortgage and several of the bills, so she had established credit—that was one good thing that her careful and unadventurous lifestyle with Doug had gotten her. Marny had seen a lot of women in Peach's position having a hard time buying or even renting after a divorce due to a lack of credit in their name.

At times it was a little disconcerting, but Peach needed this change of scenery in a big way. She needed to plant her feet in a new reality, to let ocean breezes clear her cloudy thinking, to leave all of the haunts of old Peach behind. There were too many things around that small Pennsylvania town that had reminded her of her life with Doug. And even if she had sometimes felt a slight flutter of panic at the thought of leaving behind everything she knew, she would then drive by the Nickle Plated, or see the little lot on Main where they would pick out their Christmas tree every year, or be confronted by any of a hundred other familiar places. If she wanted to be a better version of herself, she couldn't be hanging out with ghosts every day.

In the quiet moments when she wasn't dealing with the divorce, looking for where she was going to live, or writing down scenes and plot points, she would think about Ryan and wonder what he was up to. She imagined he'd moved on to another romance convention in another town, and another woman with wavering self-esteem. But even after all these weeks she still woke up with butterflies and had to hop out of bed and get busy right away so she didn't feel tempted to send him some answer to a question on his list. By now she was pretty sure any magic she'd bewitched him with had worn off anyway, and her leaving in a huff probably hadn't helped. She imagined that anything she sent now would not come back the way she wanted, if it came back at all.

It was a gorgeous late summer day when Marny met

Peach with a latte in her hand, and they drove over to Kempsville to pick up Peach's cousin Lexy for the final condo walk-through. Lexy was a curvy goddess in her late thirties with rows of wild blond ringlets and as long as Peach had known her she had two standard outfits: surf shop tees with shorts and flip-flops, or long flowing maxi dresses in tropical prints with strappy sandals. In the winter Lexy traded the tees and shorts out for hoodies and jeans with Vans. She came out to the car sporting the tee/shorts combo, and the trio headed up to Chic's Beach.

Even as an experienced real estate professional, Marny was having a hard time playing it cool as she unlocked the door of the condo. For her part Lexy was over the top with excitement, while Peach felt herself on the precipice of a whole new life. Marny strode across the living room and pushed open the curtains with a dramatic sweep, uncovering the row of French doors that led out onto the balcony and looked out towards the bay.

"Just what you ordered," she smiled at Peach. "Don't ask me how I found one so close to the beach, because I never thought I would. The stars just aligned."

"Oh Peach, this is perfect!" Lexy gasped.

As soon as Peach pushed open one of the four doors, a warm breeze blew in and drew her irresistibly out onto the balcony. It was so beautiful it was like looking at a postcard.

Lexy stepped out onto the balcony right after her, and Marny followed. They all rowed up along the railing and looked off towards the bay.

"Can you imagine having coffee and writing out here every day, Peach?" Lexy asked. "I'm gonna be over here at least once a week. Deal with it."

Peach bumped Lexy's hip with hers.

"Good. See you next week then."

She listened for the surf.

"I can hear seagulls," Peach said to herself, then turned to Marny. "I can hear seagulls, Marn!"

"We have a few," Lexy teased.

Peach looked out at the water, the sand, and her future. Everything went soft around the edges and she had one clear thought. *I wish Ryan could see this.*

Things snapped back to reality when Marny laughed and said, "When we're done here I want to take you ladies out and treat you to a celebration dinner. Where's good, Lexy?"

They took a wider walk around the condo, each of them poking into closets, running the taps, making decorating notes, discussing color palettes, and helping Peach decide which room would make the better office, and which would make the better guest room. Lexy shouted out the best places to get furniture, paint and decorations.

They agreed the kitchen was kind of small, but Peach's days of cooking big family dinners were at least on a long pause. Still, it had a very pretty terra cotta tile backsplash in at least six colors and an island that opened up into the living area. The place was nowhere near as big as her house, but it was enough space for her and for having a few friends over, and that was all she needed.

Peach's phone trilled with the particular notification for Melissa making a video call. She picked up and the other women gathered close.

"Hi honey, is everything okay?"

"Hi Mom! Yes, I'm okay."

"Marny is here too, and Lexy, we're at the new place." Peach panned the camera for her to see the place and then made sure Marny and Lexy were in view.

"Hi Aunty Marn, Aunty Lex!"

"Hi sweetie!" Marny said.

"Hi Meliss!" Lexy said.

"It's so cool to see you three together! I am calling with, well I don't know if it's good news, but it's information."

"Okay, what is it?"

"I found out who that woman is."

Peach had been so happy and absorbed for the past week she couldn't think of what Melissa was referring to.

"What woman, hon?"

"The one from the viral fake video."

"Ohhh," Marny and Lexy both said. They exchanged looks and leaned in.

"Oh shit. Okay." Peach wasn't sure she wanted to dust up all the embarrassment and other feelings right now. But what the hell.

"Her name is Angel, ironically. Angel Martin, and she lives in Irving, Texas. After looking at all of her socials, I did find something of a pattern."

"What's that?" Lexy piped. Marny and Peach looked at her. "What? This is exciting spy stuff."

They all looked back at Melissa on the little screen.

"She goes to a lot of these cons, all over the country. But she always seems to go when a particular model is going to be there."

"Really?" Peach asked. "Do you know which model she is?"

"Um … hold on a sec."

They could hear Melissa typing, her long braids fell from over her shoulder as she looked back to them.

"Ok, so every single con she goes to, she has a photo posted and some kind of book or calendar signed by Ryan Slate."

Marny gasped and Lexy looked at her with curiosity.

"Oh dear," Peach said.

Melissa wrinkled her freckled nose.

"He kind of looks like the model on the cover of your book, Mom. It looks like she was at Rambling Romanticon too, she has various photos and video snippets from the event. I didn't have time to look through all of it because I've got to get ready for school to start in a couple weeks, plus my job and my side gigs. But I will send you an email with all the links and some usernames to look up in various apps. Hope that helps."

"It might, thanks sweetie," Peach said. "Anyway, you should come see me the weekend before school starts and check out the condo. Your sister is coming next weekend to help me paint. Your brother is still in Germany, though. But that's okay. We can catch up at Christmas."

"Sounds good, Mom."

"Thanks again, baby."

"Welcome, bye-bye."

They all said, "Bye!" in unison before Melissa clicked off.

"Angel. That bitch," glowered Marny. "Do you think she did this because of Ryan?"

"I don't know. But I'm going to find out."

Lexy clapped and clasped her hands together.

"Oh, what do I get to do, Peach? I want to help!"

"How good are you with a computer and apps and stuff?"

"Honey, I'm a Millennial with a dad who was an early computer programmer. I eat tech for breakfast. There isn't a social media app I don't have on my phone."

"Fantastic," Peach said.

Marny looked at Lexy thoughtfully. "So … I need to do

some real estate social media stuff, Lexy. Can I pick your brain?"

Lexy shouldered her purse. "Absolutely. Anyway, I'm starving, and the place we want to go is Miranda's by the Bay. Love their stuffed butterfly shrimp, and the best tuna steaks you've had in your life."

SIXTEEN

Beachy Dreams

Lydia's stay was productive, if over too quickly for Peach's taste. She was her firstborn, and even though Jack came so soon after, there was always an unspoken tranquility whenever it was Peach and Lydia alone together. Over three days they painted all of the rooms in varying shades of pale aqua hues and calm beiges. Peach admitted it was kind of cliché, but she figured it was a cliché for a reason and that reason was because it was a vibe. The only exception was her writing room, which enjoyed the same pale aquas and basic bitch beiges as the rest of the house, but with one coral peach accent wall framing her new desk and computer writing area.

Soon after Lydia headed home, Melissa managed to come try out the newly finished guest room, and brought along her friend and roommate Rebecca, who had done such a great job retouching Ryan's photo for the cover. Rebecca was excited to get a copy of *Greyson Edging*, but Peach made her promise not to read it until she left. She still had a hard time talking openly about her book, particularly when people who asked weren't firm fans of erotic romance. And family? Forget it!

With the fall term approaching, the young women could only stay a couple of days, so Peach made the most of it, taking them to the beach twice and having Lexy over for a real family dinner. Seeing them together, Peach was starting to think maybe Melissa and Rebecca were more than just friends, but if so they didn't seem ready to talk about it so she let it go for now.

It had been a whirlwind of change and work for so long, Peach almost didn't notice when things actually began settling down. One day she realized her to-do list had shortened considerably, so she made a trip to the grocery store, put together a little cheese and charcuterie board, poured a glass of Virginia rosé from the housewarming bottle that Lexy had gifted her, and sat out on her new balcony in her new chair watching the sun set. She nibbled cheese and pepperoni on crackers, her little speaker playing jazz softly in the background, and wished once again that Ryan were there. She picked up her mobile phone and opened Instagram to see if he'd updated anything since Rambling Romanticon, and he had—just an hour before. She leaned forward in her chair.

It was a photo of her book next to a gray and pink tie and a glass of whiskey, all laid on black satin. Peach's heart fluttered. She clicked to read the caption.

Many thanks to Peach Kincaid for putting me on the cover of her debut novel. It's definitely spiked some interest in my older stock photos. You can find more photos in this set dynamicduos-tockphotos

There was a peach emoji and dark red heart at the end.

That was a good sign, right? A sweet little message just for her? Or maybe it just suited the subject. If she liked with a heart, would he even notice?

She saw that she was tagged in the photo and that the post had 3k likes and about a hundred comments. She hopped over to her account and saw that the six followers she'd had for ages had jumped up to 366 followers, all in that last hour. Her Instagram account had been set up by Lydia months ago, when Peach figured she needed one for marketing her book. With Lydia's help she had posted a half dozen photos, like writing in her notebook, reading a Rose Ramble romance by the pool. Her face wasn't in any of the images because she was not feeling photographable, but they came out well and she was happy with them, she just hadn't kept up with it. Now she had 366 followers—oop, make that 367, 368—which was cool, but also scary.

She scrolled back over some of his previous posts. Uggh, he was so handsome, and always looked happy. Nowhere did he post exactly where he lived, she noticed. She could only find images of him that said things like, "Ran two miles today" and a shot of his legs and shoes, or "Great day at IndieRom Readers Fest" and him holding up a book with his image on it, or a photo with another model striking a classic romance cover pose. There was plenty to look at but the whole page only gave a very cursory view of Ryan. She supposed that was by design, for his career.

She went back to the post from an hour ago and snapped a screen cap to send to Marny.

Peach: Should I heart it?

Marny: Depends. Do you want to talk
to him?

Peach: More than anything. And no, also.

Marny: Life is short. That sounds like Old Peach. What does New Peach say?

Peach: Good point. Come back and visit before it gets cold here, but after school is back in. I hear it's a lot quieter.

Marny: You gonna like it?

Peach: Maybe

Marny: I'll be there weekend after next.

Marny sent a few heart and kiss emojis. Peach swiped it away and went back to Instagram to hit the heart under the photo, while the heart in her chest pounded hard for a few beats. She closed the app and went back to her snacks and wine.

That night Peach stared at her phone and thought of sending Ryan a DM. She fell asleep imagining what she would say, then had a dream of Ryan. He was running on the empty sunny beach, wearing a pair of satiny running shorts and, it would seem, nothing under them. She was warming her curves in the sand as he made his way to her and offered to rub suntan oil on her back. She smiled up at his golden, shining body with a halo of sun all around him. He untied the back of her bathing suit, dripped warm oil over her back and rubbed up and down as Peach made happy sighs. He then worked his way down to her bathing suit bottoms and gently tugged at the waistband. Peach let out a moan and he pulled them all the way off. "Stunning," he said.

Peach squirmed on her beach blanket and felt the sun warming her bottom as he dripped a lot of oil and began to rub her cheeks with two hands. Kneading and massaging and making sexy noises. She looked over her shoulder at him as he pulled his shorts down and his cock stood out long and hard. Peach lifted up on her knees and invited him in from behind. He grabbed her hips, fingers sinking into her thick soft flesh as he put the tip of his cock to the center of her and pushed it in, a little at first and then all at once. Peach cried out. He reached around her with one of his long strong arms, found her excited clit and began to rub it while he was filling her up. The warmth of the sun, the sound of the ocean crashing, their oily skin sliding and slick —she started yelling his name right there on the empty beach, and he was yelling hers too, pounding into her as the waves surged. Then Peach woke up moaning and in a sweat, and realized that for the first time in her life she'd orgasmed in her sleep.

"Oh, Ryan *baby*!" she laughed out loud and went to turn on the AC, which she found she had set way too high to come on overnight. She couldn't get back to sleep so she lay in bed and opened Instagram again to peek at Ryan one more time. Just in case it helped with another dream. She had seven notifications and clicked on them—they all were by ryanslaterommmodel. Her heart leapt and she caught her breath. He had liked each one of her six posts, and tagged her in another post.

"Shit," she said and clicked on it. It took her to his account and there was a photo of Peach, right before the whole fire incident, sitting at the table in her Pat Benatar outfit, lit softly by candlelight. *Wow, I didn't know I looked that good,* she thought, and her insides got all squishy at the idea of him taking a photo of her just because he liked her. She clicked to see the caption.

*One of the prettiest ladies at the ball. Author Peach Kincaid at
@ramblingromanticon.*

There was so much to unpack here. She felt herself
blush and go fluttery. She smiled with deep satisfaction and
didn't pause a moment before liking the post. She went to
close the app, hesitated, then clicked on the comment
bubble under the image.

"Lucky to have met you. I hope to cross paths again
someday." she typed.

She hovered over the post button a moment, then hit it
and hastily closed the app.

"Ryan Slate," she said softly, her whole body smiling. A
small elfin laugh escaped her and echoed in the room.
There would be no more sleep tonight, she was sure. She
padded to her studio, and by the time the sky began getting
light again she had banged out almost five thousand words.

All written out, she crawled back into bed, only to be
woken at 9 a.m. by someone knocking. In her messy hair
and Stevie Nicks tee, Peach shuffled yawning to the door
and peeped out.

"Lexy?"

She unlocked the door and Lexy rolled in, bright-eyed
and chipper for an early Saturday morning, with a big paper
bag in her hand.

"Hey sleepy head, you go to bed late or sumpthin'?"

"I was writing 'til the sun came up, so yeah." Peach
yawned again. "I'm just gonna give you a key. Wait, do you
have coffee?"

"I have coffee and doughnuts from Beach Waves, just
down the road. Second best donuts in town."

"Second best? Okay, I see how it is," Peach laughed.

"Unfortunately, the best used to be K-Ville Donuts & Danish, but then they tried to become K-Ville Grille, and their doughnuts just went south. They closed two months ago."

"Oof, that is a sad, sad tale."

"Yes it is, but you'll love these, they're pretty great. I didn't know your preference, so I got a mix." She handed the drink tray of hot coffees to Peach, then followed her to the kitchen island with the doughnuts. Peach plunked down a roll of paper towels and some small plates and popped open the box to survey the offerings.

"Oh my god, is that a raspberry jelly with powdered sugar?"

"It is, help yourself."

"I'll do half. Do you want cream and sugar for your coffee?"

"It's all in the bag, Sugar. Here."

They each cut off a piece of doughnut and stirred their coffees—for Peach light and sweet, for Lexy just sugar.

"Thanks for coming by Lex. Feel free to bring me doughnuts any time you like. Even second best."

"I also brought you this." Lexy held out a newspaper. "It's *Virginia Beach Vibing*, all about the arts events and stuff in the area. I thought you might like it. Anyway it has a few writing organizations and book events in there, too."

Lexy slid it over and Peach started leafing through.

"There's a romance writer event here three weekends from now, with local writers. It's a small one, looks like about twenty names listed. I know it's late for you to sign up for it, if you were even ready to do that Peach, but I thought you might like to go at least—they have tickets still available. Only twenty bucks. I'd go with you."

"That sounds great. I'd love to." Peach found the page that featured the book event. It didn't have a lot of info, just the location, which was a hotel, and the time, which was 11 a.m. – 6 p.m. No parties or panels, just a simple author showcase and signing.

"Also, Gemma sent over some purses. Nice ones, designer bags. She's a little more masc these days and she was going to donate them anyway." Lexy plopped her cotton tote onto the table. "She thought you might like a look first. She knows you got rid of a lot of your old stuff."

"That's so thoughtful. Thanks, Gemma."

Gemma had been Lexy's partner for the last six years, which wasn't always easy in conservative-leaning Virginia Beach. Especially during the pandemic, which only seemed to embolden anti-vaxxers, anti-maskers, and anti-anything people in a really unfortunate way. But Lexy and Gemma had managed to carve out a little community for themselves, where several of their like-minded friends own businesses and they all supported each other.

Peach wiped the powdered sugar from her hands and peeked inside.

"Oh my god, is that a Gucci?"

"Yeah, there are a couple Guccis in there, and I think a Coach, too. Enjoy. Just donate what you don't want."

"Be sure to tell Gemma thanks. Maybe yinz can come for dinner soon?"

"Yinz?" Lexy laughed. "Damn, haven't heard that in a while."

"Oh, shoot," Peach laughed. "Yeah, I slip up sometimes. A lot of people still say 'yinz' up where I used to live." It felt weird to say it out loud, *where I used to live.*

"Do you say pop or coke?"

"Usually soda. I haven't actually said pop in a while. I think coke is more of a southern thing, though."

Lexy looked thoughtful over a bite of glazed cake donut.

"Yeah, I guess that tracks. I get all three around here. My friends are from all over."

Peach finished off her coffee and tried smoothing down her crazy hair while she contemplated the doughnut box. There was a Boston cream lurking in there.

"So, Peach?"

"Yeah?"

"You ever gonna tell me what this Ryan Slate stuff is all about?" Lexy lifted an eyebrow.

Peach blushed and gave a sheepish grin.

SEVENTEEN

Socials

The pair spent the rest of the morning setting up every kind of social media app Lexy thought might be worthwhile, and she gave Peach a cursory lesson on each one, as well as some wise cautions.

"Lurk for a while and watch other people, so you don't fuck up. Because if you fuck up, it's out there forever. I'm not trying to scare you, but the internet can be a brutal place. Well, you already know it can also be a deceptive place. Jesus, when I saw that video I almost flew out to see you."

"It's bad enough to have somebody target me like that. But seriously, I'm not sure a romance writer can have a career if all people think of when they see her is 'never trust a fart'."

Lexy let out a belly laugh. "Oh my god, Peach!"

"I need to find out why that woman did it. And I need people to know it's fake. It can't be legal to just smear somebody like that! Can it?"

"Of course, you could always just let it pass."

Peach looked out of the window into the bright day, looking contemplative.

"Yeah, I suppose …"

"Right? You could just let it … pass." Lexy stifled a grin, until Peach poked her in the ribs.

"Fuck that."

They poked around all over socials and the internet and gathered as much info as they could on Angel Martin, including one of those $29 basic background checks. The results were slim:

Angel Martin. Unmarried. Has lived in Oklahoma, Nebraska, and Texas. 28 or 29 years old. Two charges DUI, 7 years previous. No children.

Not much to go on. Then Peach noticed a little arrow link:

"This person may have more court documents to look at. Click here to buy this information."

"Whattya think, Lex? Should I spend the $12?"

"Hell yes!"

"Oh, okay. I thought I might be getting too sucked in."

"Well, then we both are. Click it." Lexy leaned in over Peach's shoulder as the records came up.

"Oh damn," Peach murmured. She had to scroll three pages to see it all.

"Holy shit, Peach. Well that sure explains a lot!"

"It certainly does."

EIGHTEEN

Beauty and the Beach

Over the next couple of days Peach hunted down every scrap of anything that looked problematic on Angel's socials. She downloaded all of it, put it in a file and Dropboxed it to her lawyer. He said it may take a day or two to get a cease and desist order, but that it would be done before the weekend. Peach knew that nothing could fully undo the damage this woman had done to her, but she was going to do her best to make sure she didn't keep getting away with this kind of shit.

Having sent the documents off she treated herself to a chai latte at Castaway Café, claimed a spot on their sunny patio, and tried to write, but she was too distracted. She opened her phone and peeked at Instagram to see if Ryan had posted anything new. He hadn't. Her heart sank. She'd hoped for some word, some news of him. It was a very Jane Austin mood, longing for a letter like this. At least that sounded more sophisticated than "schoolgirl crush."

After some poking around on various romance tags she found a con Ryan happened to be at this past weekend in Ohio, seen in posts from a model, a reader, and two authors who had him on their covers. She wondered why he didn't post more about where he was going to be. If only he would, she could try to get tickets and catch a glimpse of him—from afar of course. Because she really wasn't ready.

Keep telling yourself that kid. Not being ready is only a heartbeat away from not being able to help yourself.

She reached into the side pocket of her bag and slid out the well-thumbed list.

Things I would like to know about Peach Kincaid:
Favorite color or colors (just one can be so limiting)
Favorite flower
The perfect date night
The perfect birthday celebration
Favorite comfort food
~~Favorite band (or top three, if it's too hard to choose)~~
~~First concert and favorite concert~~
If you won the lottery, what is the first thing you'd buy just for yourself?

She ran her fingers over the handwriting. She snuck a quick look around, held the paper close to her nose, and inhaled. It still retained a small amount of his scent, and vividly brought him back to her. She sighed and leaned back in her chair, letting the sun warm her face.

Peach heard the owner of the flower shop next door push open her green wood and glass door, and she opened her eyes to see her set a large bucket of peach colored roses on the outside display table. It was already overflowing with wildflower bouquets, elegant single peonies in five colors, joyful daisies and asters, and a variety of carnations, but the abundant roses were what caught her eye.

The woman saw Peach watching and waved at her, then tucked her hands into her bright pink apron pockets. She took a couple of steps over.

"Do you like them?"

Peach smiled. "They're absolutely gorgeous. Such a pale peachy color."

The woman, probably in her thirties and wearing bright pink lipstick and a pixie cut, wagged her finger and took a couple of steps back in her blue Keds to tug one of the peach roses from the bucket.

"Here, it looks like you could use a rose."

Peach knew her face was going red—her pale cheeks always gave her away. She smiled and her whole face lit up.

"Oh my gosh, I really could. Thank you!"

Now that she was closer, Peach could see the woman's nametag read "Danny." Danny gave a little bow.

"It's called a Just Peachy Champagne Romance rose. I'm glad it gave you a smile. Have a lovely rest of your day."

Peach watched her disappear back into the store. She gave the rose a sniff and it smelled strong and sweet but not too cloying. She laid it on the teak tabletop and used the portrait setting on her phone to take an up-close image of the bloom. She opened Instagram and posted the photo with a caption:

My new favorite flower, the Just Peachy Champagne Romance rose. Danny at Peaseblossom & Mustardseed flower shop in Virginia Beach gave me one to cheer me up. It worked!

Her heart skipped a few beats when she hit "post." She didn't bother with hashtags or tagging the store. This post wasn't for that. She was sending a message out to the whole world that was meant for just one person.

She clicked open her pen and crossed off "Your favorite flower."

Peach took a deep breath, sighed, and had a sip of her now-cold latte. Within ten minutes her phone sent a notification from Instagram:

ryanslaterommmodel liked your post

Her tummy did flops and she floated on cloud nine for the rest of the day.

Inspiration struck. At the grocery store she picked up everything she needed to make homemade pizza—fresh soft mozzarella, a basil plant, tomatoes, red onions, olive oil, garlic bulbs. She went home and called Lexy to come over for late pizza and a movie.

In the meantime Peach changed into a low-cut black blouse and pushup bra, put on her "Kiss the Chef" apron with magenta lips, and shot videos of herself making the dough and patting it out into a pizza. Doing her best Nigella impersonation, she seductively (but subtly) cut up soft balls of mozzarella into slices, drizzled on olive oil, and laid fresh basil down on top with thinly sliced red onion. She wasn't sure quite how to look sexy sliding a pizza into the oven, but she gave it her best shot.

Lexy arrived in one of her shorts and surf shop shirt pairings. She put Peach to work right away showing her how to edit and post a video on Instagram, and Peach added a heartfelt caption:

Fav comfort food? Homemade pizza! In particular I use my homemade dough, soft mozzarella, fresh basil, thinly sliced red onions, and kalamata olives. And you could only call it comfort food for me if I get to make it! There's something about making pizza from scratch that really helps me stay present and calms me right down. Also, I make this pizza for all of my favorite people. What's your favorite comfort food?

Again, no hashtags were needed, because this post also was meant for just one person. But waiting for her phone to signal that this person had liked it was as bad as waiting for a guy to call for the second date. Peach was on pins and needles, peeking at her phone out of the corner of her eye while they watched *Dirty Dancing*.

"God I miss Patrick Swayze," Lexy lamented, biting into a hot gooey slice. "Holy shit, this pizza is amazing."

Peach smiled. "I know. It's probably the thing that Doug misses the most about me."

"Fuckin' Doug." Lexy bit into her pizza again and then washed it down with red wine.

It was before anybody tried to put Baby in a corner, while Peach was only on her second slice, that she saw her phone light up with notifications.

ryanslaterommmodel liked your post

Then a surprise second one came in right after.

ryanslaterommmodel commented on your post

Peach's heart went up into her throat. "Shit!" she said. Lexy paused the movie and turned to her.

"What, did he like it?" She wiped her fingertips on her napkin and leaned over to look at the phone. "Oh shit, he liked it *and* commented! That is some hella romantic shit, Peach."

Peach was kind of frozen. She sat there, mouth open for what seemed like forever, until Lexy finally prodded her.

"Well?"

"Well what should I do?"

Lexy chuckled and snorted. "You should open it! Lordy woman!"

As Peach went to slide her phone open, another notification came in.

ryanslaterommmodel tagged you in a post

Both women gave a loud "Eeep!" at the same time.

Peach stared, caught like a deer in the headlights. Lexy waited, eyes on her cousin, until she could wait no more.

"Uggh! Peach I'm gonna scream if you don't open it."

Peach gripped the phone tighter and squeezed her eyes closed.

"What am I doing? What the hell am I doing? This is not real. He was an amazing weekend and if I try to make it more than that, it's going to get all ruined."

"Sweetie, look at me."

Peach opened her eyes and turned toward her.

"It's already more than that."

Peach let out a big sigh and nodded.

"Do you imagine these feelings are going to go away, Peach?"

Peach shrugged. "In time maybe. Probably."

"With no regrets?"

Peach looked at her again. "Well, maybe some regrets."

"Does New Peach want to start her journey on the regret path, or the adventures path?"

Peach murmured, "Adventures."

"No, no. Happy, excited! Like this: Adventures!"

"The ink isn't even dry on my divorce papers yet. My heart wants it, but my brain is telling me to stop being so … so …"

"Passionate?" Lexy raised a knowing eyebrow.

Peach didn't reply, she opened the phone and first went to the comment under her pizza post. Lexy leaned in close and they both read it.

ryanslaterommodel: Pizza is my favorite comfort food too! I hope you make that pizza for me someday.

He followed it with a red heart and a pizza emoji.

Peach hearted his comment but looked confused for a moment.

"Do you think the heart is for me or for pizza?"

"You, dummy."

"Well, I don't want to presume."

"You should presume. It's more fun. Click over to his page so we can see what he tagged you in."

They both were, without realizing it, holding their breath. There was only one new post since the one about her book that he'd posted and it was a doozie. It was a shirtless Ryan lying on black satin sheets, a book open and tented on his chest and he's smiling at the camera. It's Peach's book.

"Oh my," Lexy said. "He's very good-looking. I mean if I was playing for that team I'd be all over that. Damn."

"I'm scared to look at what he wrote. You read it out to me."

Lexy pried the phone out of her hands and clicked on the image.

"Shew boy. Okay, it says: page 136."

"Okay …"

"Okay."

Peach looked at her cousin. "And …?"

"And nothing, that's what it says."

Lexy showed her the phone and Peach squinted at it. They looked at each other and both of them hopped up and ran over to the bookshelf. Peach snatched up her book and started flipping pages.

"Okay, okay. Here it is. It's the start of a chapter so there's only one paragraph on it."

"Well, what's it say?"

Greyson was glad Bella came for a visit after so many months. He'd longed for those dark sparkling eyes to fall into, and her long red lily-scented hair to tangle his fingers in, and the sound of her soft sighs next to him in bed. She gazed at him and her smile was one of want, so he took Bella's hand and led her out to the balcony that overlooked the ocean. With the waves crashing and the stars winking down on them, he slid her sundress up and over her head and lay her down on the platform covered in bed-sized silk and linen pillows. As Bella watched, Greyson loosened his tie, then unknotted it and slid it off, unbuttoned his shirt and kneeled down next to her.

"Oh wow, I remember that part. It goes pretty well for Bella. Well, for him too. I really liked your book, by the way."

"What do you think it means?" Peach asked.

"I think it means he wants to make you naked by the beach at night and recreate the scene in the book."

"Maybe it just means he likes the scene, I mean for me as an author. You know, he just likes the book."

"Girl you are thinking this to death. Why don't you just text him? Or better yet, you're Gen X, call him!"

"I think he's an Elder Millennial."

"Then text, but do something. He likes you! Like, he *like* likes you." Lexy put her hands on Peach's shoulders and looked her in the eye. "I promise."

"Okay, I'll … I will post the rest of the things on his list this week. If he's still interacting with me, I'll text and ask if we can talk on the phone. But …!"

Lexy gave her some cautious side-eye.

"But what?"

"If I get my heart broken, you have to promise to be my emotional support lesbian."

"Deal. Now let's watch the end of this movie, then I need to get home."

NINETEEN

Haters Gonna Hate

The next morning at 8:32, Peach woke to a video call notification warbling insistently. She struggled to rise, squinting at the sun pouring in over her cream-on-cream seahorse quilt, and groped for her reading glasses. They were becoming more and more necessary, just to see who was calling her. It was Melissa.

"Hi honey, is everything okay?"

"I'm okay. But that Angel person posted another video, and you should go take a look."

Peach sat bolt upright, her heart beating harder, and she started to sweat a little.

"Now what?" she asked with a small note of panic.

"It's okay, Mom—just more fake stuff. Let me know if you need anything, but I'm on my way to preregister for next semester. Love you."

"Okay, thanks honey. Love you, too."

Peach thumbed the TikTok icon and went to Romance-ConGoer4eva's account, where the most recent video still was an image of Peach at Rambling Romanticon. It looked like a legit image of her standing behind her table. She swallowed hard and clicked on the video.

There was a young woman, early twenties probably, standing at her table, and Peach recalled she'd asked if *Greyson Edging* was in the library. She recognized the rainbow tutu skirt and the tee tied in a knot at the waist with a graphic of a pile of books on it. She remembered her mostly for the tutu and for her gum smacking and the weird face she made at Peach when she told her it wasn't in the library yet. The girl had spun, flipped her hair and walked away. Peach had called after her, "Probably by the end of the year though." Peach didn't think there could be anything too damning in the video since the interaction was brief and innocent and Peach was nice to her the whole time.

She clicked it and, like the fake video of her on the plane, the quality was surprisingly low. The clip showed the girl asking, "Is your book in the library?" But instead of Peach replying "It's not available in the library yet, I'm afraid," what she heard was, "Don't be cheap, buy a book if you're going to come to these things." Then the girl spun around and flipped her hair and walked off looking pissed, which Peach hadn't seen in person because her back was to her.

Peach blanched. She looked at the counter on the video. It was just posted late last night and already had 40k views and 28k likes. She called Lexy and Marny on a group video chat and told them what was going on. Both of them told her to call her lawyer as soon as they hung up.

She downloaded the video and uploaded it to her attorney's DropBox, then called his office saying it was an emergency. Her lawyer told her that he could probably have the video down by the end of the day, and that they should begin the process of suing her immediately. Peach agreed and let him get to his work.

Her stomach was in knots, but she still clicked around to see if anybody had stitched or reposted it and a bunch of reader and author accounts had started to shred Peach to bits. On the one hand, she could understand why they would. That influencer was a part of their community, Peach was not. She so badly wanted to post a video addressing the two fake ones, but her lawyer told her not to, so she refrained. But it was hard seeing so many people say such nasty things when they didn't know anything about her.

Peach decided to close out the app and try to forget about it. It was out of her hands. It wasn't like she had a big career as an author, she was just getting started, so thankfully not many people knew about her. She didn't have any more appearances scheduled at this point, and she doubted anybody would accept her anyway. Besides, she couldn't show her face at an event until this was sorted out.

She knew why Angel was doing what she was doing, but the animosity still made Peach sick to her stomach, and the fact that the woman had made her a target was unreasonable and unfair. But reason and fairness don't come into play when somebody is obsessed.

Peach spent the next hour walking the beach for her heart health and some calming endorphins. She met Lexy to have some ice cream and farm-to-table food at a little place that everybody had to wait in line for on the weekend, but was much easier to get into on a workday. Peach was not ready to be alone with her thoughts so they dropped into a local artists' cooperative for a bit before Peach headed home.

The quiet there was much too loud, so Peach turned on

the Bee-Gees and poured a big glass of wine and tried to relax on her balcony. Still, she couldn't resist opening Instagram. Even though she hadn't gotten any notifications, she just wanted to see if Ryan had posted anything else. Earlier she was too worked up and hadn't hearted the post he tagged her in. Now she was worried he saw the latest fake video and might never want to speak to her. She went ahead and liked his post anyway.

Ryan hadn't posted anything new in the last couple of days—maybe he thought she didn't like his post because she didn't hit that heart button right away. Or maybe he was so busy he didn't notice. Or maybe he was at a con right now, wooing some other middle-aged woman who was trying to have her glow-up. Peach had a vivid impulse to hurl her phone off the balcony.

After two fishbowl-sized glasses of wine she pulled Ryan's list out and looked at it. She went to Marny's Facebook page and after some digging she found the photos from a trip they'd taken to London eight years ago. There was Peach, standing in front of the most charming little bookstore called "Plume & Print" in her white pinup dress with little blue forget-me-nots all over it. Wearing a little blue pillbox, and carrying a round baby-blue patent leather purse that matched her shoes and belt, she had felt like a million bucks that day, and that store had reminded her of the bookstore in *You've Got Mail*. She smiled at the image and copied it to her photo album, then opened Instagram and uploaded it. She wrote:

> *If I ever win the lottery I'm buying myself a cute little book-store wherever I live.*

Book emojis, heart emojis, and ... post.

Three days without an Instagram notification from Ryan. He hadn't posted anything new either. She told herself he was busy working and then took her laptop to the coffee shop, where she intended to work on the next book she didn't plan on publishing any time soon. If ever. Maybe her reputation would never recover—maybe her books were just for her.

Decaf mocha in hand, she opened the laptop and checked her email. There was a document from her lawyer showing that Angel Martin had received her second cease and desist letter, that she was told to remove the videos immediately, and she had been served with court papers to sue her for slander and libel, since she also wrote some very uncomplimentary and untrue things about Peach in her post caption and her comments.

Checking Angel's account, she saw she had taken down the videos, but the most recent post was an image of the cease and desist order with some parts blocked out, and plenty of people had already stitched it. Some commented that Peach was clearly trying to control the narrative because she was embarrassed by her bad behavior in the library video, and others were saying they thought it might be fake. Some of them were arguing how they could understand her first video being just plain embarrassing, but the second one was the antithesis of booklovers. That libraries were the bedrock of literacy and she should be glad to have a book in the library and that not all authors get that privilege—all of which Peach agreed with. She would love to have her book in a library. She didn't say any of those things. This AI stuff was getting out of hand. And apparently it was totally okay to lie until somebody could legally challenge you.

Worse, Peach found she'd been tagged in multiple Instagram posts about the topic, and the whole thing was spreading. She really had gone viral, and for none of the good reasons an author would want to. Her career was over before it started.

She closed out the social apps and the email, and opened her latest work in progress, the one she'd started back at Romanticon, *Desire Therapy*. She worked on it through the evening, only stopping for potty breaks, fresh mocha lattes, and snacks. Once the sun dipped below the town buildings the temperature dropped, and she hadn't thought to bring a sweater, so she packed everything up and walked home, where she worked until she passed out in bed.

Peach woke to a dead laptop and smudged eyeliner. *Girl, you are too old to be falling asleep in your makeup*, she scolded herself. *You need to keep up that skincare routine.* She shuffled into the bathroom and took a long shower, dried her hair, and put on her makeup, feeling like it was kind of pointless the whole time. Still, she did feel more like she could take on the day once she put herself together. She made avocado toast, drank a bit of juice, and headed right back to the coffee shop patio to get her favorite drink and work on *Desire Therapy*.

More notifications kept pinging in so she turned them off and put her nose into her work in progress. By dinner she'd managed another 6k words and she did that over and over for the next eight days, until she was able to type "The End."

She couldn't believe it. She'd finished her second book, and nobody even knew about it. She wasn't sure now if she wanted anybody to know about it. Maybe it wasn't worth anything beyond just her knowing she did it.

Some good news came in her email that same day: they had reached a settlement agreement with Angel Martin a few days ago. She was ordered to remove any and all content related to Peach Kincaid and any future pen names, and put up an apology video that tells what she did and why. The video had to be posted on all social media platforms she shared the original posts to by Friday at 11:00 a.m. EDT, which was tomorrow.

Despite this triumph and possible reversal of fortune, Peach had a lingering sadness that Ryan hadn't liked her post about the lottery, even though she knew that most of what was between them was in her imagination. Lexy was wrong—he liked her, but he didn't *like* like her.

As she was getting herself a dozen congratulatory Just Peachy roses from the flower shop, Lexy called.

"What's up?" Peach answered as she scanned her card and waved goodbye to Danny. She cradled the roses in her arm while she walked and talked to Lexy.

"Hey, how's your day going, Peachy?"

"Pretty great, actually."

"Really? Did you hear back from the lawyer?"

"Yes, Angel has agreed to never post about me again and to put up a video admitting what she did. I doubt she'll say it's because she's obsessed with Ryan, but you saw the background check. That's one hundred percent why."

"You know what they say, haters gonna hate! Anyway, that is good news. It won't erase it all from the internet, but it should make everybody in the romance world aware. Speaking of, don't forget, that romance event is the day after tomorrow. You're still coming right?"

"Well, I suppose by then the word will be out that those videos are fake and I will at least be able to show my face, so, yeah."

"Great! I'll pick you up at ten, we'll grab a doughnut and coffee and head over."

"Sounds perfect. I'm getting the jelly, even though it's going to mess up my makeup."

"Bring a little touch-up kit, it's worth it."

Peach wasn't ready to share that she'd finished her book. She wanted to savor the victory all on her own for a bit. But also she didn't want anybody pressuring her, even with good intentions, to publish it.

She went home, texted Marny about the legal victory, then clipped the roses to stand in the hopeful vase she'd bought when she moved in. All the vases she used to own were left in Pennsylvania, because all of them held the ghosts of Doug and Old Peach. This new vase was a deep aqua clear glass and went perfectly with the delicate peach of the roses.

While it was true that virtually no one knew about *Desire Therapy*, the book was no longer entirely secret. Peach was excited enough about it that she finally decided to go ahead and send it off to her editor and cover designer. Then she celebrated her victory by curling up with hot tea and an *Outlander* binge on the couch, snuggled under the quilt of old baby clothes her kids had had made for her fifty-second birthday last September. One year ago next week. She was about to turn fifty-three.

Jesus, fifty-three! There was a time she thought that was ancient. Nearly dead. People expect you to know everything once you're in your forties—how to navigate relationships, how to never get duped or conned, how to know liars from honest people. But you don't. If you're an honest person, a liar can definitely still fool you. And if you hadn't had a variety of interpersonal relationships, you might not know how to process them. Being over fifty doesn't protect you from bad actors or mistakes any more than being twenty or thirty. The only thing you can really do is choose to be trusting or distrusting, and it was hard to always know which one to go with, even now, at almost fifty-three.

Since the second video by Angel, and Ryan's continued radio silence, Peach had largely shied away from socials. But now, riding high on her good day and knowing that Angel's apology video was going out tomorrow, Peach was feeling a little braver. She dug in the hall closet and pulled out the paint chips for her décor colors, and snapped a photo of the aquas and corals fanned out. She took a photo of the roses in the vase. Then she settled back into her seat under the quilt and posted a carousel of the two images, the floral arrangement being the first slide and the paint chips second. She wrote:

I don't often think of myself having favorite colors, but these keep coming up over and over.

She hit the share button and tried to ignore all the notifications since they likely had to do with the Angel video. Right now, she understood why people were upset, but after tomorrow if they were still harassing her, she would start blocking them.

A text from Marny came in:

Marny: That's great about the videos. I also noticed that Ryan liked your lottery post. You can cross it off the list. I followed him, and he followed me back. Does that make us all practically family now? When's the wedding? (wink emojis and hearts)

Peach: He did?! I didn't see it. All these people were tagging me in posts about those fake videos so I shut off my notifications. Love you! Please come for my birthday next week if you're available. The beach will be getting cold soon.

Marny: He did! Yes, I'll come! Love you, goodnight!

Peach: Night!

Peach went straight to Instagram and checked her lottery post. There were a few nasty comments she deleted but ten likes on the post. One of them was Ryan. She smiled and let out a squee like a schoolgirl. Sleep was going to come a little easier tonight.

TWENTY

The Apology

The next morning Peach decided to not look at her phone until she'd had breakfast and gotten some writing done. Instead of the coffee shop, she opted for tea and the balcony, and dove into book three. She could hardly believe she was on book three! Last year she barely imagined she could finish book one. She still wasn't entirely sure she would put these book babies out into the world, but she had another book in her and she was going to write it, dammit.

Book three would be the second in the series about billionaire Greyson Caine and his beloved Bella Edwards, and it would be titled *Greyson Dominating: Shades of Passion Series, Book 2*.

Peach couldn't tell if it was her imagination or she really was getting faster. She flew through 5k words before lunch and decided to take a break, have some fruit and cheese and maybe sip a glass of wine. By the time she got her snack together she realized it was nearly noon and the apology should be up.

Steadying her breathing, she picked up her phone, opened TikTok and went to the RomanceConGoer4eva account. There was a video up. With all the shit that went wrong before yesterday, she was nervous this would go sideways too, but when she clicked on the video she saw a contrite Angel Martin looking a bit worse for wear. Peach was still mad that it took legal action to make her take her slanders back. How many other people had she done this sort of thing to who didn't have money for a lawyer? Peach had some sympathy for her as a person who was probably suffering from an undiagnosed or untreated mental condition, but what Angel did was potentially ruinous to Peach's career. And it was cruel.

Peach opened the video.

"Hello, I'm Angel and I'm the owner of this account. I am extremely sorry for the videos I posted about Peach Kincaid, they were fakes. I want to apologize to Ms. Kincaid and to all of my followers for my actions. I had the videos altered with AI and my friend helped me shoot the second one by being in the video and asking Peach Kincaid a question that was innocent sounding, but I had an AI film editor alter it. I was jealous that Ryan Slate seemed to be interacting with her a lot at Rambling Romanticon and I wanted to embarrass her. I know my actions were not only unkind, but unethical and they breached the trust of my followers who count on me to be honest. I also know some people saw the cease and desist video too and there will be conspiracy theories about all of this, but I accept that I did wrong here and I'm grateful that Peach Kincaid did not press charges against me. I'll be closing my account down and taking a break from social media for a while. I hope all of you can forgive me. Please keep reading books and sharing about the love of reading."

Peach closed her phone and set it down. The girl looked rattled and contrite and the apology was adequate. Peach didn't fully trust it was going to undo all the damage, but at least she felt like she could show her face in romance circles again. She munched on grapes and went to her bag to pull out the list.

Things I would like to know about Peach Kincaid:
~~*Favorite color or colors (just one can be so limiting)*~~
~~*Favorite flower*~~
The perfect date night
The perfect birthday celebration
~~*Favorite comfort food*~~
~~*Favorite band (or top three, if it's too hard to choose)*~~
~~*First concert and favorite concert*~~
~~*If you won the lottery, what is the first thing you'd buy just for yourself?*~~

Just two left. She took down her mermaid wall calendar and circled September nineteenth with blue marker, drew a little birthday cake in the square, and took a photo. She opened Instagram—still ignoring the mountains of notifications—and posted the photo with a long caption:

I've had a lot of nice birthdays, some were just cake and dinner at home with the family, others were drinks with friends and karaoke. My favorite was a pirate themed one with lots of decorations and my own custom cocktail Peach's Cherry. I once planned a trip to San Francisco for my birthday, which was an amazing family vacation, but it ended up being a lot of work for me. I think for 53 (yes, 53!) I want a spa day, and to eat seafood next to the beach and drink pina coladas while wearing something beautiful I bought myself. That sounds so indulgent, doesn't it? What would you do for your birthday?

Peach hesitated for a moment because the internet had been so busy eating her alive lately, but she wasn't going to let a bunch of angry people with the wrong information interfere with the first big romance of New Peach's life.

Post.

Not long after, Lexy rang.

"Hey Lex. You saw the apology video?"

"I did. It seems good. How do you feel?"

"I'm okay. It'll all pass at some point I guess. The fact that it is so out of my hands and beyond my control, in some ways that's helping me deal. I read the paperwork from my lawyer. Angel Martin had heard about my little incident on the plane, the real one, the minor one, from the guy who was at the con and on the plane with me. There was never any video on the plane, and it was all hearsay, so both her videos were total fabrications."

"What a way to learn all about AI though, aye?"

"I'm tellin' ya. But one thing's for sure, I'll never leave home without antacid. And I will not eat for two hours before anything that makes me nervous! Sheesh! Anyhoo, see you at ten tomorrow. Looking forward to it."

"Me too! And you should take some video for your socials!"

"Oh boy, well, I either need to be in or out on the socials I guess. We'll talk about it later. Love ya."

"Love you, too."

Peach wrote for the rest of the day and again after dinner. By the time she crawled into bed she had a pretty good start to her third book and a very sore neck.

TWENTY-ONE

Yes It's a Meet Cute, Really

When Peach got up she dressed to impress. She wanted the other authors to take her seriously, especially after the video fiascos. She wore a peach colored wrap dress and taupe Mary Jane heels with an adorable vintage flair. She'd found them at Macy's on clearance and for once they had a wide shoe she actually liked, so she bought them in black, too.

She applied a nice day-makeup with a nude lip and rosy cheeks. Peach hadn't settled on a perfume yet because she wanted something different from her old citrus body spray, so she dabbed some vanilla extract behind her ears and on her wrists. Something fancier would have to wait, but she still felt sassy and very put together. Going through the purses that Lexy had brought over she found a cute beige and taupe Coach bag that worked well with her dress and shoes. At a minute to 10:00 Lexy knocked and Peach let her in and did a little twirl in the foyer.

"What do you think of this bag with this outfit?"

"Damn, that's perfect."

"I know. Okay, I'm just about ready."

"Hurry up, all the good doughnuts will be gone."

Peach dumped her purse into the Coach bag, grabbed her keys off of the hook, and off they went in Lexy's white Subaru.

First they stopped at Beach Waves Bakery and Lexy treated them both to a doughnut and cup of coffee. The place was packed so they chatted about family things and didn't stick around long. Peach had to tidy a little powdered sugar off of her cleavage, but other than that, a touch up of lip gloss and she was all good.

They pulled up to the hotel and found plenty of people there as well. Lexy had the tickets, so after they worked their way into the lobby, Peach moved to the side and waited for Lexy to grab their passes. She also came back with swag bags and instructions about when and where lunch would be and what time things ended.

"This is really cool," Lexy said. "I mean, I know it's small, but it's pretty cool."

"I wanted to tell you how much I appreciate you trying to get me out and back on the horse. I'm not as nervous as I thought I would be. I doubt anybody here knows me, and I didn't recognize any of the names on the author roster, so I'm probably safe."

"Good, glad you're feeling up to it. How's your book going? The Desire one?"

In that moment Peach made the decision.

"Promise you won't make a big deal, okay Lex?"

"What? Why?"

"Because I need you to promise to not make a big deal right now. We can later, just not now." Peach raised her eyebrows and waited.

"Okay, I promise," Lexy said.

"I finished it. Two days ago."

Lexy's eyes widened and Peach could tell she was winding up to be loud and excited. She held up a finger and whispered sternly, "You promised!"

Lexy put her hands up as high as her shoulders and whispered back, "Yay."

Peach gave her an affectionate eye-roll.

"Let's go check out these authors."

They stopped at each author's table and one or the other bought a book or picked up cards. If any of the authors recognized Peach, they didn't let on, and by the lunch break they had a tall stack of books to chat about while they ate.

Lexy and Peach made their way to the hotel courtyard amid the crowd of authors and other attendees. They stopped at the buffet table and picked up shrimp cocktails, mini-quiches, and chocolate dipped strawberries—apparently this was a regular theme at romance events. They found a table and set down their plates and books, and Peach decided she was ready for a cocktail from the cash bar.

She couldn't help a small laugh when she told the bartender, "I'll have a Sex on the Beach."

"You got it," he said and reached for a glass. "That'll be $10."

Peach set her perfectly coordinated bag down and started digging through everything she had dumped into it for her wallet, which was of course buried at the bottom. She gave the wallet a tug and her purse went over.

Fortunately, not much flew out. Unruffled, she said "Oops" and "I'll have it in a second" while she stooped to grab a lipstick, a box of mints, and an earring that was trying to roll away.

As she stood up, she heard a man say, "I'll get her Sex on the Beach."

Peach gasped and her eyes went wide. She turned around to see Ryan standing there smiling, holding out cash to the bartender and looking as dashing as ever, this time in a three-piece suit and striped tie.

Peach's heart started pounding. The murmuring chatter around them went silent.

"You! How?" she heard herself splutter.

The bartender held out the drink, but Peach didn't notice it. Ryan laid the money on the bar without taking his eyes off her. She stepped towards him, weightless. Phones came out and started clicking and recording. Peach went up on tiptoes and put her arms around his neck, and their lips met.

Everything and everyone else faded away for those moments they pressed together, their mouths remembering each other, their tongues reunited in a slow dance. He smelled so good and tasted even better. Their long kiss ended, she looked in his smiling eyes.

"How the hell are you here?" she said quietly. "Are you real? Am I dreaming this?"

"Very real. As real as it gets."

"You weren't on the roster. I would have known. Everyone would have known. I mean, you are a draw." She smiled crookedly. "Don't let it go to your head."

"I called them yesterday and asked if I could be a part of the event. A surprise mystery guest or something. They couldn't say yes fast enough."

"Why? Why here?"

"I saw your post about being in Virginia Beach."

Peach was back down on her heels again, though their hands were still clasped. She was looking up at him, not quite connecting the dots.

"The flower shop?" he supplied.

"Oh, right."

"And I figured there was a good chance you'd be here."

"So you're sleuthy too."

The sounds of people talking started to rise again. Reality came back online and Peach laughed quietly.

"I'm glad you're here, Ryan. Really glad."

"Can I take your drink to your table?"

"You can."

Lexy traded looks and excited whispers with Peach as they made their way back to their table, Ryan walking suavely behind with drinks in his hands. The crowd seemed to part around them, and there was a lot of picture taking and hushed talking, but she was getting used to that. She figured this was how her life as New Peach was going to be —she could embrace it and make the best of it, or curl up and hide in her little chrysalis. But she knew she'd never fit in that old thing again.

So Peach held her head high and strutted to her table, the handsome Ryan Slate trailing her, watching her bottom sway back and forth with a big smile on his face.

After a quick hi-and-bye introduction, Lexy grabbed her bag of books and scooted to another table, and Peach didn't argue with her. Her focus was on Ryan, and as she admitted to her cousin, she had it bad for him. She nibbled on shrimp, drank her Sex on the Beach, and he fed her a strawberry. When everybody else started drifting back to the event, they stayed put, keeping their perfect bubble of low conversation—Peach hooking her foot around Ryan's calf and rubbing up and down slowly, Ryan smiling big with his hand on Peach's knee.

"What if this is a mistake?" Peach asked, though with a dreamy grin still on her lips.

"Then it's one I want to make," Ryan declared, and leaned in and pressed his mouth to hers for a moment.

"Want to see my condo? I have a king-sized bed."

"I would love to see your condo. Right now. Carry your books for you?" He reached out and stroked the back of her bare arm. A shiver ran through Peach. She could feel her nipples bump out under the silky peach fabric. Gooseflesh crept down her neck and torso. He picked up her book tote.

"Wait, Ryan, aren't you supposed to make an appearance or something?"

He laughed softly.

"I just did. Weren't you taking pictures like everybody else?"

"Oh, riiight." She giggled. Then she laughed out loud, and slipped her arm into his as they started walking to the parking lot.

"Are we taking these to your car, dear lady?"

"No, I came with Lexy. Oh, Lexy! I'd better text her!"

She opened her phone and saw one message.

> Lexy: omg girl, u r living the dream! Go get him! CALL ME L8R!

Peach replied with a row of hearts and dropped the phone back in her bag.

"So I guess we're going to your car, then?"

"That's it over there," he said, pointing to an aqua blue Mercedes. "It's only a rental."

He opened the door for her first, then set her books in the back and climbed in the driver's seat. He turned over the engine, plugged in his phone, and the sound system came to life with the Bee-Gees singing "How Deep is Your Love."

"Stop. Is this my real life?" Peach crowed a triumphant "Woohoo!" as Ryan drove off.

She directed him for the twelve minutes and four turns to get back to her apartment, all the while swaying and singing along to Seventies love songs, the windows down and the salty September air breezing through, the fingers of Ryan's right and her left hand laced together.

She opened her front door with a flourish. "Please come in," she said.

"I could never refuse an invitation like that from you, beautiful lady."

"I'm sure there are others you couldn't refuse it from as well," she teased.

He put his arms around her.

"About that … I had a blood test done last week. Just in case I'd be seeing you again. I'm all clear." He gently kissed her forehead. "I'm not trying to make you big promises, Peach, but I am saying, you are all I've been able to think about. And the only one I want to be with."

"I think about you a lot, too." Her voice got quieter. "I feel like I'm on the edge of very good things. Not that my family, my kids, all the things I did before weren't good, they were just … different. The good parts."

"The good parts," he repeated back. "I'll bet you're an amazing mom."

She hugged him and stepped out of his embrace and opened the fridge. She held up a wine bottle and gave it a wag.

"Fancy a glass?"

"Sure."

"My kids like me," she said, pulling down some stem glasses. "When your kids are grown and they still like you,

you know you've done a half decent job." She pulled out the cork and began to pour. "Do you have any kids?"

"I don't. Never settled down for very long. I like kids, just never saw myself with them. But I do like my mom, so as a son I can relate to that."

"What about your dad?"

"He died when I was little. The flu, of all things."

She came over and handed him a glass, looking in his eyes.

"I'm sorry to hear that, Ryan. Really."

"Thanks. My mom was pretty independent, but she was sad a lot, too. I tried to be the man of the house and look after her but, you know, I was little. Now I take care of her in different ways. Call every week. Send flowers from time to time. She's a busy lady—it's not like she needs me to give her life purpose or something. And smart. She's a professor. She says she'll never retire."

"Well I'm impressed. What does she teach?"

"Greek Mythology and Women's Studies." He slipped off his jacket and hung it over the back of a dining chair.

"Sounds like a pretty cool lady. Won't retire, huh?" Peach laughed. "Good for her! How old is she?"

"She turned sixty-three this past February. She's one of those lucky Valentine's babies."

He unbuttoned his vest and slid that off too, and hung it on the chair as well.

Peach felt her face go cold and a mild panic rise.

"Sixty-three? Your mom is only ten years older than me, Ryan."

"Okay," he said. It was too plain for Peach's liking.

"Just, okay?"

"Yeah, it doesn't matter." He unbuttoned his cuffs and

rolled up his sleeves and leaned there on the counter close to her body. Looking all relaxed and tasty.

"Huh." Peach contemplated this for a moment and realized that anybody she dated might have a mother that didn't seem all that much older than her, or a daughter not much younger, and there was no real point in worrying about that dynamic right now. She decided to put the whole question out of her head, and took a long sip of her wine.

"I am curious though, how did you find out about this particular romance event?"

"It would have been more surprising if I *hadn't* seen it. There were posts from at least four authors that I've attended events with before. I'm pretty plugged into the community."

"So you saw my post about the flowers, put two and two together, and voilà, you're here. For me."

He touched her chin with his thumb and bent over and whispered his warm breath right into her ear, "For you."

That shiver again that he was so good at sending through her.

"So, are you going to show me the bedroom?"

She didn't answer. She took another sip of wine, took his hand, and led him.

"I've never had a man in this room before."

He pulled her hand up to his mouth and kissed the back of it.

"I'm honored, milady."

She laughed. "I love it when you say that. I don't even care if it's corny."

She could feel a frenzied passion rising from her center —for this man, for this life—and she didn't want to resist it any longer. She set her glass on the dresser and bent to unbuckle her shoe when he knelt by her foot.

"Allow me?"

She pointed her toe and he worked at the tiny buckles, first one shoe, then the other. She watched him down there, the top of his head and that thick shiny dark hair with sprinkles of gray, his rolled up sleeves exposing his sexy forearms. Everything about this man was sexy. If they were together a while she supposed she'd eventually find some not-so-sexy things, but at this moment New Peach wasn't going to think about that. New Peach was taking a bite of this ripe fruit and letting the juice run down her chin.

She stepped out of her unbuckled shoes and Ryan stood and slid his off as well, setting both pairs to the side. He stood tall in front of her.

"Would you loosen my tie?"

He raised his large hands and ran them from her shoulder blades to the small of her back while she loosened his tie and slipped it from his neck. She tossed it toward the dresser where it landed on the lampshade.

She started unbuttoning his shirt, his spicy, smoky smell delighting her, and she felt the warmth of him radiating all around her as he gently held and kneaded her hips. When she got to the button just above his waistband he tugged the bottom of it free, unbuttoned the rest and whipped off his shirt. Peach thrilled at the sight of his naked torso, resting her hands on his pecs and leaning in to kiss the center of his chest.

Ryan tangled his fingers in her hair, cupping her head in his hands as she kissed and nuzzled him. Their mouths met and they helped each other peel off their clothes, pressing close, not wanting to let a splinter of light between them. Embracing, caressing, tossing garments and undergarments until they were both naked, their arms surrounding each other, they shared the deepest most sensual kisses that Peach had ever experienced.

They pulled apart only long enough for Ryan to sweep away the seahorse comforter, revealing ivory satin sheets. He laid back on the bed, his cock erect against his body. Standing above him, naked, round, and soft, she felt like a goddess of love as Ryan reached a hand out and beckoned her.

Peach crawled across the bed to his lap, raising a plush thigh over his hips. He pushed back his cock so it was standing tall and she lowered herself slowly, slipping him into her an inch at a time. His long cock was filling her up, and when she settled her hips she felt him deep inside her.

Ryan moaned and cupped her breasts as she rode him, rocking, grunting, groaning in their primal connection. She panted his name over and over as her want swelled and surged, and louder as she climaxed, with Ryan saying hers as he bucked beneath her, both of them wanting to stay inside of each other, deep and slow and always. Peach rode that wave hard until it floated her back into shore, with Ryan quaking and pulsing inside her, both finally sated.

She hung there a moment, her breasts swaying in front of him, and he couldn't resist giving them gentle pets and kisses. Then he put his arms around her and pulled her chest to his and they lay that way in a sort of worshiping embrace for a long while.

They wrapped themselves in satin sheets, sipped white wine and nibbled fruit, made pasta and made love, and talked long into the night, learning about each other, imprinting on each other, until 4 a.m., when they both could no longer resist the sleep that had been trying to take them.

TWENTY-TWO

Book Slut

T he lovers woke hungry and happy, another sunny late summer day setting the vibe. They decided on eggs, toast, and bacon and Peach got started on a pot of coffee. Ryan looked over the books Peach bought and told her about the authors he knew and what they were like. He was friendly with all of them but one, Tina Tassell, who apparently doesn't do well with the word "no" but is otherwise a decent sort. As he described them, the romance crowd seemed to be a pretty supportive bunch. Peach was hoping that would translate to not having to be embarrassed over the fake videos anymore.

The bacon was sizzling quietly in the oven while Peach warmed up her iron skillet and Ryan hunted down bread for the toaster.

"Also, do you have any orange juice?"

"I do. Try the other fridge door."

"Ah. Got it."

Peach didn't want to get too far ahead of herself, but this was nice. It was really nice. And she kept waiting for the other shoe to drop, but it didn't.

Ryan opened the balcony doors to let the breezes in, and together they set the table. When everything was ready they dug in, both of them famished. It might have been the best breakfast Peach had ever eaten.

Their hunger sated, they lingered over the remaining scraps and made conversation. Peach poured herself more juice and munched on a piece of extra crispy bacon.

"Did you believe those videos about me?"

Ryan put down his fork and bit a corner off buttered toast.

"What videos?"

"Seriously? You didn't see the videos?"

"Well, I thought it might be better if you thought I never did." He laughed and finished the toast in two more bites.

"I see." She looked at him out of the corner of her eye and smirked. "It might've been at that. But seriously, when you saw them, why didn't you warn me that the girl was stalking you?"

"I actually only saw the one about the library a couple of days ago, and I knew right away it was fake. It sounded nothing like you. Then someone reposted Ms. Martin's apology yesterday and I realized you must've already handled the situation. Amazingly well, I might add. The other video, I only heard about."

He finished off his juice and stood up and put his arm around her, gave her a squeeze and kissed the top of her head.

"I'm sorry you got tangled up in all that. I don't really post where I am or where I'm going to be on my socials anymore because of this sort of thing. In fact I largely avoid them now because of people like Angel Martin, who I've blocked in every way I can think of. She's the worst one, but there are a few others."

"Why don't you take out restraining orders or something?"

"I will with her now. I don't want her bothering you, and I'd like to be able to post my events again. She's never done anything this far out before."

"All the trouble she had to go to to make this happen, it's just crazy."

"Don't worry Peachy, I'm on it."

He gathered up the dishes and started rinsing them and putting them in the dishwasher, and she watched. It was one of the sexiest things she'd ever seen in her entire life, that delicious man doing dishes in his underwear without her having to ask. He could walk around in his jockey shorts all day as far as she was concerned. A very different experience from seeing Doug slouching in his two-times too big boxers and striped tube socks. Which Peach always had to launder. What it must be like to be with a man who takes care of his own laundry.

"We were talking about hometowns earlier? I live in Baltimore, so I was pretty close to home at Romanticon. My mom's tenure is at University of Maryland." He looked over his shoulder at her as he slid a dish into the washer. "Go Terps."

She laughed.

"I mean it, I sweat Old Bay."

She laughed again. This was so nice and comfortable. So gently sexy. So achingly sensual.

"Is that where you went to school?"

"I actually went to the College Park campus. I have a degree in ... wait for it ... philosophy."

Peach felt a little outclassed. Again.

"I am impressed, Mr. Slate. I went to Carnegie Mellon

in Pittsburgh, but I dropped out in my third year to get married and start a family. Is that disappointing?"

"Not to me," he said as he closed the dishwasher and dried his hands. She was memorizing everything she could about him, in case this whole thing evaporated. His hips, his ass, his pecs and shoulders. But also his neck, his earlobes, his eyes and cheekbones, the places on his head where his hair goes flat when he sleeps. His smell. His laugh. The drawl of certain words, and the clip of others. She wanted to remember it always.

"I loved your book, by the way."

"Stop. You're just being sweet."

He took her face into his hands and looked down into her bright sparkling eyes.

"I mean it. I wouldn't lie to you about that."

"Thank you."

They kissed only briefly, but it sent electricity to every corner of her body. His too—she felt him growing hard and she smiled and pressed the palm of her hand against him. He drew in a sharp breath and leaned in for a longer kiss.

Her phone rang. She tried to ignore it but it paused and rang again, a video call. She peeked over and saw it was Melissa.

"Oh no."

He pulled back from her touch.

"What's the matter?"

"Every time my daughter calls lately something horrible is being spread about me on the internet."

"Sounds like you'd better answer it then."

"I always answer when my kids call, but the last few calls have all been Angel-related."

She lifted the phone for a better face-to-face view and answered.

"Hi honey."

"Hi Mom."

"Melissa, is everything okay?"

"Yes, actually. I'm happy to say that it is."

Ryan smiled and said, "That's good news."

Melissa tilted her head, "Who's that there while you're still in your Stevie Nicks shirt?"

Peach made an "oops" face.

"Um, that's my friend … Ryan Slate."

She turned the camera a little, being careful to tilt upwards, and he waved at her.

"Hi Melissa."

"Hel-lo there."

Peach turned the camera back to herself.

"Woah, go Mom."

"So what's this not-bad news?"

"Go to TikTok and put your name in."

"Oh no." Peach was crestfallen. She didn't want to be the subject of people's videos ever again.

"Just do it. It's okay, I promise. Love you and … um … have fun."

"Love you too, Peanut."

Peach closed the phone and pressed it facedown on the table for a moment, as though she could keep the internet trapped inside it.

"Great, another video. She said it's not bad, but it's probably not good either. I'll settle for not embarrassing!"

She gave him a sheepish face and sighed and picked the phone up again. He stood behind her and slipped his arms around her waist, looking over her shoulder while she searched her name on TikTok. Only a couple of the old videos came up now, probably as stitches or other people recording them showed up. The rest showed a young blonde woman in a pink shirt that read "Book Slut" in crystals on the front.

"Oh shit, I know her," Peach said.

"I recognize her, too. Katie is her name, I think. She goes to a lot of romance conventions. She's a pretty big book influencer, like 250k followers."

"Oh man, imagine the damage she could do. That other reviewer didn't have half that many."

"Don't be scared. I'm here. Just click play and we'll deal with it together."

She looked up at him over her shoulder and he kissed her nose. She turned back to her phone and hit play.

"Hi all! Katie Book Slut here and I wanted to talk about a book by an author whose name has made the rounds here on booktok. You may know Peach Kincaid from those horrible fake videos that went out, and they tore through the whole romance book community like wildfire. Everybody was talking about the videos, but nobody was talking about her book. I bought the book because one of my favorite models Ryan Slate is on the cover."

She held up the cover and tapped it with her long pink glitter nails.

"My TBR shelf has been mad at me, so once I finished off my first two books of September I slid in *Greyson Edging*, the first book in a series written by Kincaid. Y'all this book was so good. You know I love a spicy book and this one has the spice, the connection, the romance, the happy ending. It has it all. I loved it and if you like this kind of romance, you're missing out if you don't pick it up. Happy reading from your favorite book slut! If you like this tee, you can get it in my shop. Link below."

TWENTY-THREE

Happily

After seeing about twenty responses and hot takes on Katie Book Slut's video, plus a few captures of Ryan and Peach at the romance book event yesterday, they put down their phones and agreed on a shower. They washed each other tenderly, with lots of soapy, warm caresses and one round of Peach kissing and stroking Ryan's cock until he came. Then after the shower there was a round of Ryan drying her off, then kissing and humming on Peach's most tender places until she came. They both were positively glowing.

They went for a walk on the beach and stood there quietly hand in hand, watching the waves crashing as they rolled in.

"I finished my second book and started a third," Peach said. It felt more real, now that she said it to him.

"Peach, that's wonderful! Congratulations! We should get together with your friends and celebrate."

"I'd love to."

"I could stop by for a visit on my way down to Raleigh

Sexxxy Romance Con in two weeks. We can have dinner with however many people you want. My treat."

"Do you have to go back to Baltimore before Raleigh for something?"

"Well, I might not, but that's not so long, is it? I could come down the day before and spend it with you."

Peach stopped walking. She turned to Ryan and laid her head on his chest.

"What I'm asking is, would you stay with me for those two weeks? Or is that … too much too fast?"

There was a beat, a moment's hesitation. Peach trembled just a little as Ryan pulled back. Then he gently lifted her face to look in her eyes.

"Don't you see? I can't get too much of you. I can't get enough of you. I'll make arrangements. There's no place I'd rather be than with you."

Peach touched his face.

"This is my perfect date night," she said.

"Mine, too," he said, and scooped her up in his arms before they headed back to the condo.

~~The perfect date night~~

The End

Epilogue

Ryan Slate and Peach Kincaid went shopping the following day so Ryan wouldn't have to go all the way back to Baltimore for two weeks worth of clothes.

Their first few days together were all fucking, all the time. In every room. At any time of day or night. They barely wore clothes, walking lazily around the condo, eating grapes and chocolate, sipping Prosecco and getting each other worked up again and again.

By the fourth day Peach would have liked a giant block of ice to sit on, she was so tender and overheated, and Ryan was glad for a break himself. Far from cooling their connection however, it gave them time to do all kinds of other things. They read a book out loud together, went on a photo safari with Peach's new camera, tracked down various diners around the region and stopped in a few local bars to listen to music and have a beer.

Peach was feeling more alive and juicy than she ever had. And Ryan, though always friendly with women who flirted, found his devotion to Peach was undivided. He told her so, the evening he brought back two dozen Just Peachy Champagne Romance roses.

The week following the post from Book Slut, Peach's book went viral in a big way. She eventually sold almost 150,000 copies, which made her lightheaded whenever she thought of it. She eagerly signed up for next year's Rambling Romanticon and half a dozen other book fests and cons. She was really, officially, undeniably an author, and believed that maybe there was a space for her in Romancelandia.

On the nineteenth of September she got her birthday wish. Marny came to town, and she, Lexy and Peach all went for massages, facials, manicures, pedicures, and fresh hairdos. Before dinner Peach slipped on a new bias cut silk dress in grass green with a slit up the side and little bell sleeves, finished off with a pink shrug and sandals. Along with Gemma and Ryan, they all went to Claire's Oceanside Tavern and sat out on the patio, enjoying seafood and piña coladas and finally a chocolate truffle flight with PEACH written in chocolate syrup on the plate.

Later at the condo they enjoyed a delectable coconut cake Gemma made, played Bee-Gees music and told stories and spilled tea about the goings on in Virginia Beach and back in Beaver County, Pennsylvania. Lexy pulled up the local pet shelter website and they all oohed and awed over the dogs, everyone chiming in on what sort of puppy Peach should get.

Peach woke up every morning to Ryan's face, and even if he hadn't been as stunning as he was, she would have had all of the same feels that were filling her up. And not even a hint of anything that resembled a red flag.

Ryan headed off to the Raleigh Sexxxy Romance Con on a Thursday. They made love all morning and then she watched him drive away in his rental Mercedes, waving him goodbye in her new Stevie Nicks shirt he got her for her birthday, while under that was a delicate gold figaro chain he'd also surprised her with. She wondered if maybe it was a sweet parting gift, and that would be the last she'd see of him, but down deep she knew better, and he came back to Virginia Beach the next Monday and stayed another week before finally heading back to Baltimore.

They spent the last two days of that week figuring out where all Ryan's books and records were going to go in the condo.

Acknowledgements & Thanks

There are so many things that go into a book. A kind word from a reader, or a preorder, can turn a bad writing day around and make it feel like you are doing something worthwhile. Thank you to everybody who has been supportive or somehow played a role in my writing. Thanks also to the bookish, booktok, and romance community at large—you help keep me going when "comparitis" kicks in and tries to drown out the creativity.

Also of note is that I got the idea for this book in response to Michelle Fewer inviting me to Charm City Romanticon 2025. Michelle is a huge champion of romance authors and makes some space at her event for authors that have a smaller backlist, like me. I am working on it though!

Love and thanks to my sister Brandi, who I swear one day will be on my team full-time, because she's so supportive and she's just that good, which is why she tends to be the alpha reader for my projects. I know, I advise people not to turn to family for this kind of thing, but if you happen to be lucky enough to have a sister or cousin like her, feel free to ignore that advice.

Love also to my daughters Amber and Jade, who have always wanted me to dream big and be the best, happiest me I can be. They are the best part of me walking around in the world. And to Robin, my "adopted" daughter, who slides in and saves the day and inspires little scenes in several of my books—just look for anything to do with a firefighter, and some part of Robin is there.

This is the first book I have written without the loving, occasionally pesky presence of my dear Abyssinian cat Kali. I didn't realize how much she was my emotional support animal until she was gone. Fortunately we found Salem, our fluffy black rescue kitten, and he does a good job of trying to fill her paw prints. It is also the first book I've written since my daughter had a baby, and so as a proud gigi I want to say I love you Henry.

Huge thanks to Candice/Cardyn for being the most pragmatic yet kind friend ever, full of wisdom and cheer and also my partner in various bookish happenings big and small. She is one of the first people I think of when I need a creative solution to something, and whenever we get together I always feel so happy and rejuvenated.

And as always, to my editor, best friend, and writing coach Will Hardy, my small-town cinnamon roll—you're the best and I love you.

About the Author

H.L. Brooks is a lover and weaver of fairy tales. Her subjects range from star-crossed lovers who change into werewolves to feisty witches solving mysteries to steamy erotic fiction—all with an emphasis on strong female characters of various ages and body types.

She originally hails from a dead steel mill town in Pennsylvania, the daughter of a U.S. Marine Vietnam War veteran and an artsy mother. H.L. is feminist, sex-positive, body-positive, chatty, and curious. She has an affinity for 1970s and 80s fashion and nostalgia, which is reflected in her stories. You can read her sensual observations and micro-fiction in the Sensual Sunday series at her blog, www.hlbrooks.com, where she also muses about life and posts news about upcoming events.

H.L. is the founder of The Write Women Book Festival and The Write Women Network group, hosting diverse and inclusive author salons and book events for women. She is a member of Maryland Romance Writers, Maryland Writers' Association, Hampton Roads Writers, Women's Fiction Writers Association, and Pennwriters.

H.L. is a fan of cats, dogs, fun socks, love letters, chocolate, and tequila. She enjoys old-house living in a small town, isn't sure if ghosts exist—but isn't ruling it out—and is the biggest fan of her editor and partner in all things Will C. Hardy. You can find her on Instagram, Threads, and

TikTok as @hlbrookswrites or at her website, www.hlbrooks.com

www.ingramcontent.com/pod-product-compliance
Lightning Source LLC
Chambersburg PA
CBHW070451120726
47910CB00003B/1002